Kristen –
hey girl ♡
being such an awesome
friend and fan ♡
Best of luck with
your writing! –jm

KNIGHT'S END
JAMI MONTGOMERY

JMontgomery

All characters and events in this work are purely fictional and are not meant as actual persons or events. Any resemblance to real persons or events is accidental.

No part of this publication may be reproduced, stored in a retrieval system, or transmitted in any form or by any means, electronic, mechanical, photocopying, recording, or otherwise, without written permission of the publisher. For information regarding permission, write to Jami Montgomery, Attention: Permission, at jamimonty@gmail.com.

This book was originally published by Dreams Come True Publishing as an ebook.

Copyright © 2012 by Jami Montgomery
All rights reserved. Published by Dreams Come True Publishing.

Cover design by Laura Lawrence

First Printing, April 2012.

Dedication

There are so many people whom I could thank for making this book a possibility. First off, I have to thank the community of friends I found during my time at inkpop. The kind words, the helpful suggestions, and the support I found there has been unmatched by everything else in my life, and without them, this book would not be where it is now.

I wish I could thank everyone personally, but a few names will have to do. To my mom, Tina Montgomery, for always supporting me, letting me read things to her that I loved or wasn't sure about, and always offering opinions when I needed them (and even when I didn't). Thank you for always believing in me, believing I would get there, and letting me try crazy things to make it.

To my sister, Megan Montgomery, for reading the first draft of Knight's End and for doing all the right things in all the right places. You cried when I wanted someone to be sad and laughed when I tried to be funny. For that, I am eternally grateful.

To Mandy Springer, for going through the entire novel with me and making sure my historical aspect was accurate, as well as letting me know my sentence structure was horrible, thank you so much. Without you, my characters would probably be eating hot dogs in Tahiti, and I can't thank you enough.

To the people I haven't mentioned here, you know who you are. Thank you for sticking with me when this book was really (really) rough and not worthy of eyes. Thank you for making suggestions, pointing out my grammar errors, and letting me know which characters needed work and which were fine. Thank you for following this book from rough draft to finished and printed. Without you, Aston and Jade would just be characters on a computer screen, sitting down waiting for me to make their lives worth something like all of you have done to mine. I can never thank my readers, my friends, or my family enough for all they've done for me. But this book is my attempt at telling everyone just how much I love and appreciate them.

    I hope you enjoy this story I have to tell. Happy reading.

Jami Montgomery

TABLE OF CONTENTS

ONE 5

TWO 15

THREE 21

FOUR 27

FIVE 35

SIX 43

SEVEN 51

EIGHT 57

NINE 63

TEN 77

ELEVEN 87

TWELVE 91

THIRTEEN 105

FOURTEEN 113

FIFTEEN 125

SIXTEEN 131

SEVENTEEN 143

EIGHTEEN 153

NINETEEN 165
TWENTY 177
TWENTY ONE 189
TWENTY TWO 201
TWENTY THREE 211
TWENTY FOUR 225
TWENTY-FIVE 222

Prologue

Adrenaline had gotten him this far. Now that he was here, the rush was leaving, fear taking its place. He could feel his heart pounding in his chest as his mind raced. *I can't let anyone see me,* Ernst thought, pushing a stray lock of ebony hair out of his eyes. *They won't understand.*

He continued down the darkened palace corridor, the moonlight filtering through the tall windows lighting his way as he stalked through the shadows. The plush runner beneath his feet softened his footsteps, almost completely masking them as he passed painting after painting on the grey stone walls. Turning right at the end of the corridor, he followed the map he'd laid out in his head earlier that evening. Past three more doors, he found the one he'd been looking for.

The dark oak door with torches on either side looked like every other; the rose engraved into the wood showed it for what it really was. This room held royalty. Inside, he knew it would be clean and organized. That was how Prince Orion liked his room, kempt with no indication of his dishonorable habits. The prince liked to frequent Azazel's brothels, taking as many women as he wanted. He was oft violent with his women. The ones who didn't cooperate and complained ended up missing, then dead.

Ernst curled his lip in disgust.

You can do this, Ernst. You've killed plenty of men in battle. Why should this one life be any different? Taking a deep breath to calm his nerves, he carefully pushed the door open. He stepped inside and closed the door behind him, letting it click softly into place. A quick look over his shoulder showed him that nobody had stirred.

Silently, Ernst crept to the bed, the light from a candle on the bedside table guiding him. Prince Orion rested there, nestled under the blankets. Wavy red hair was strewn across his pillow. His right arm crossed over his chest, his left arm trapped underneath the woman in bed beside him. She wasn't important to Ernst; she was nothing more than a woman Orion had coaxed off the streets. The woman would be in for a surprise in the morning.

Ernst pulled his ruby-hilted dagger from his belt, nearly dropping it from his sweaty grip. His father had given the dagger to him as a gift when he'd killed his first stag. Now, Ernst intended to complete a different kind of hunt, one that wouldn't make his father proud. The clock struck midnight, chiming twelve times, echoing throughout the palace.

Don't think about it. Just do it. Ernst set the blade against Orion's throat. He held his breath and drug the dagger against the prince's neck, digging into the soft flesh. He left one long, narrow cut, jumping back as blood sprayed from the wound before settling into a steady, pulsing flow.

His heart leapt into his throat when Orion's brown eyes flashed open, locking on his own emerald ones. The prince let out a gargled cry before his life left him, his eyes staring at the ceiling.

That was all Ernst could take.

Time to leave. Ernst took off out the door, no longer worrying about staying hidden. He momentarily tripped over the outstretched leg of a guard he had killed earlier, but he caught his balance and continued through the palace. He heard a woman's scream and knew Orion's woman had awoken. Cursing under his breath, Ernst continued down the hall, momentarily pressing himself behind thick curtains as soldiers stormed toward the prince's room.

As soon as the soldiers had vanished down the corridor, he continued his escape. He took a sharp left at the end of the hall and ran into one of King Damien's soldiers. The man muttered a quick apology before noting the blood covered dagger still clutched in Ernst's hand. He reached to draw his sword, but before he could call for help, Ernst shoved the man against the stone wall behind him, crushing his palm against the knight's throat. He thrust his dagger under the man's ribcage, watched his eyes dim, and let him drop to the ground.

The obstacle out of his way, Ernst exited through the palace doors and ran to the stables, careful to stay hidden in the trees' shadows and avoid patches of moonlight. He reached the stable and mounted his horse, grateful that he'd tacked him before going to Orion's room. He quickly steered the palfrey out the open palace gates. King Damien always kept them open, in case anyone needed aid in the middle of the night.

After tonight's events, that would probably change.

The murderer made it into the forest before he had to stop and heave. He jumped off his horse just as his stomach twisted, emptying itself of its contents. Seeing men die in battle was natural for him. Murdering a man in his bed was more than he could handle. When he finished retching, Ernst wiped the back of his hand across his mouth. If he truly planned to carry out his mission, he would need to gain a stronger stomach.

These men deserve their fate. They are cruel men in positions of power, men who should be changing the world instead of making it worse. I'm the only one who can get rid of them. I'm the only one who isn't afraid of them.

Ernst climbed back on his horse, turning the animal toward home. Prince Orion's death would bring chaos to the five adjoining kingdoms. He wanted to make sure he was home before accusations started flowing freely from the mouths of the monarchs.

"Every new beginning comes from some other beginning's end."

- Seneca -

Six Months Later

One

He'd never been summoned without reason before.

Aston was on his way to a meeting with King Donn. As he walked through the empty corridor, his nerves danced. His cobalt eyes rested lightly on bronze suits of armor lining the walls before darting away again. Thick strands of dusty blond hair stuck to his face as he sweat, and he kept his fists clenched at his side.

The knight set his wandering eyes on the pine doors at the end of the hallway, currently gaping open and waiting for him. When he reached the doors, two stoic-faced guards bowed him in. He acknowledged the bows with a slight nod before heading into the throne room.

As the grand doors sealed behind him, he started for the three solid gold thrones at the far end of the room. Two of them were occupied by King Donn and Prince Talbot. The knight held his head high as he made his way down the long red velvet carpet, stopping at the king's feet. Aston bowed low, taking a knee.

"Your Majesty," he said, grateful his voice didn't waver. The monarch nodded to him, and Aston stood, waiting for his orders as he studied his king.

The king looked less than royal, lounging in his throne. His belly rolled over the top of his pants and his ruby red shirt did nothing to hide the pouch. King Donn's pants were wrinkled brown cloth, one leg tucked into a black boot while the other was left out. His hair was slowly disappearing, leaving little more than an unkempt silver flap on the top of his head. The king's face was grim, his grey eyes somber as he looked at Aston.

"It has been half a year since Prince Orion was murdered. The murderer, The Rogue Royal, is still at large and has found another target. It seems the man is never satisfied. How many kills does that make, Talbot?" King Donn asked, looking at his son.

Talbot looked away in annoyance, swatting a fly from his shoulder before answering. "Duke Aeron would make twelve, Father." He slipped down further in his chair in a practiced slouch, his dark eyes looking everywhere but at the knight.

"Eleven, then. King Aric of Adion received a letter early this morning announcing the Rogue's intent, as is customary. I want you to take Talbot with you and go to Adion. My old friend, Duke Aeron of Northsbury, is arriving there with his wife tomorrow afternoon. The Rogue intends to strike there, at midnight. I want you to stop him. You haven't been formally invited by King Aric, so make sure you aren't seen. It would seem uncouth of me, sending a knight to protect the duke at another man's castle." Donn waved his hand, as if to dismiss Aston, but the knight still had questions.

"Sire, if it is uncouth, why send Talbot and I?" Aston questioned. It was unlike the king to care about other people more than he cared about appearances.

"Duke Aeron has been a close friend of mine for ages, and I fear King Aric is getting soft in his old age. The man will most likely ignore the Rogue's warnings. I want someone there to save Aeron," the king answered, looking down his nose at his knight.

His tone was condescending, and Aston felt foolish. He shouldn't have questioned his king.

The knight nodded, setting his eyes on the man who was to accompany him. Prince Talbot's brunet hair curled to his ears; his brown eyes were so dark they were almost black. The prince currently wore a shirt so golden, Aston wondered if it were inlaid with the precious metal. His black pants were neatly pressed, his ebony shoes shining in the chandelier's bright light.

Brooding and snide, the twenty-summers-old male was undoubtedly the worst prince ever to grace a kingdom. Talbot didn't care about his people; he loved the riches that came with royalty, and could have done without the duty.

Aston sighed. It would doom him, bringing Talbot along; something was bound to go wrong. But the knight knew he had no choice. He couldn't turn down a direct order from the king.

"Yes, your Majesty. When would you like for us to ride out?" Aston questioned.

"As soon as you are ready," came the king's reply. King Donn dismissed the knight with a wave of his hand. Aston nodded, placing his hand across his heart before turning and leaving the room to prepare.

**

Talbot stayed behind, waiting until Aston left before turning to his father.

"Why do I have to go with him, Father?" Talbot whined like a child. His father sent him a stern look, but Talbot didn't back down. "Why not send William or Robert? Send another knight and let me stay here."

Donn shook his head. "You *will* accompany Aston. I know I can trust you with him. The other knights don't like working with him. He's the best at what he does, but they say he is too kind, too gentle. Too willing to forgive when an enemy surrenders. I need you there to make sure that what needs to be done is *done*."

"But Father, think of the danger! Say we do save the duke's life. What happens if the Rogue decides he wants to kill someone else in the duke's place? Someone like me?"

"Oh, don't be so dramatic, son. The Rogue has a clear target. If he doesn't kill the duke, that better mean he won't kill anyone again." The king made a slicing motion across his neck, and the prince understood. His father wanted The Rogue Royal out of the picture. Permanently.

"Yes, Father," Talbot sighed, still not wanting to go. He knew his father would not change his mind. The prince stood slowly and sulked out of the room, not bothering to throw his shoulders back and stand tall as he walked through the palace. He didn't care about appearances. Right now, all the prince wanted was a warm bath and a warm bed. He wouldn't get either until Aston and he returned home from their mission. He found the knight at the end of the hall, talking to a cook. He scoffed and went to interrupt the men's conversation.

"Oy, Aston!" he called, putting on a fake smile. Upon seeing the prince, the cook bowed and left. Aston turned to face Talbot, what looked like a forced grin plastered on his face. Talbot stood a bit taller than Aston, his eyes placed mere inches above the two-meter-tall knight's. Aston had to look up slightly to meet the prince's eyes; his height was something Talbot had always admired about himself. He liked making people look up to him. It made him feel more superior to them.

"Prince Talbot." Aston bowed before standing at attention again. "What do you need?"

"I wanted to go over the details of the mission with you. We will ride out when I feel we are ready and not before a proper meal. We will ride cautiously and, when we arrive, you will make camp while I supervise," Talbot announced, counting off on his fingers as he made his conditions. "Oh, and we will not rise before sunrise to start toward Fridel again once the mission is complete. I need my rest." Having made his demands, Talbot turned on his heel and headed toward his chambers, leaving Aston standing there clenching his fists and grinding his teeth.

**

"I despise that man," Aston muttered to himself. He turned and headed in the opposite direction, going down two flights of stairs to the knights' hall.

His room was messier than usual. Clothes were strewn across the floor and over his wrought iron bed. The quilt he used at night hung halfway to the floor, the pillows turned sideways. He had just returned home from a mission the day before and hadn't gotten around to cleaning yet. In his twenty- two summers, Aston had never been the neatest person in the kingdom.

With a sigh, he grabbed his half-unpacked bag from the floor, emptied the rest of the soiled clothes from it and proceeded to grab everything he would need. After packing, he left his room again and went to the mess hall to find supper while he waited for Talbot. He caught sight of his closest friend in the palace, a young man who was currently training under the head housekeeper. It was unusual for a boy to be a maid, but Richard was barely thirteen summers old and too small to do anything else. Not to mention the fact that he was horrible at every other job.

Smiling, Aston made himself a plate of food and then headed towards the long, wooden table where Richard sat by himself. The boy looked up and smiled when Aston sat beside him, but quickly went back to shoveling food into his mouth.

"Slow down there, Richie. You're going to make yourself sick," Aston said, laughing before filling his own mouth with food.

"Madam Louise said I had to eat quickly and then get back to work. I've been told your chambers are filthy, Sir," Richie answered. Aston nearly choked on his food, but he recovered and patted the red-headed boy on the back.

"Good luck with that woman. She's tough as can be but she'll do good by you. As for my chambers, I have been away nearly a fortnight. I've just returned, but I have to leave again. I don't have time to clean. That's what *you* are for." Aston noticed the frown that marred the boy's face upon hearing his favorite knight had to leave again. He seemed to ignore the part about cleaning being his job.

"Where will you go this time?" Richie asked.

"To Adion, the most beautiful country around! You would love it, Richie. Stone houses, yards full of blooming flowers, a bookshop with hundreds of books, and beautiful women around every corner." Aston winked at the young boy, knowing he didn't care about women.

"A bookshop, sir! Would you bring me a book back?" Richie's hazel eyes lit up at the prospects.

"You know I will, Richie. I always do," he replied. He took another bite of his beans and a quick bite of bread while he waited for Richie's reply.

"And you'll teach me to read more too, right?" Aston nodded. "Thank you, Aston." The boy smiled and went back to shoveling beans into his mouth. They spent the rest of the meal in silence, but it wasn't uncomfortable. Richie was one of the few people he called a friend.

"I must go now. I'm bringing Talbot with me and I'm sure he's already waiting at the stables," Aston said, finishing his bread. Richie's freckle covered nose crinkled at mention of the prince.

"You have to bring Prince Talbot?" the boy whispered, moving in close to Aston and covering his face with his hand. "But he's so mean."

The knight smiled at the boy. "Yes, Richie, I have to bring the prince. Maybe he will be helpful."

Richie's face quickly turned skeptical. "I doubt it, Sir. Just watch his feet. He likes to kick people."

"Only you, Richie. He only bothers you." At Richie's confused expression, Aston elaborated. "It's because you are small. He thinks he can intimidate you."

"But it's not just me! It's all of the maids and cooks and stable hands and--"

"Okay, Richie, okay! I'll watch his feet," Aston said, laughing as the boy continued his list. Richie nodded, seemingly satisfied, and went back to eating.

With a quick ruffle of the boy's hair, Aston bade Richie farewell and went back to his chambers to grab his satchel. He took one last, longing look at his bed before heading toward the stables.

The white building came into view as soon as Aston walked out the castle's front doors. The stable was tall with a dozen wooden stall doors on two sides. An open hallway ran between the two rows of stalls, ending at a wall made for tacking horses. A door to the right of the wall led into the tack room, filled with saddles, bridles, and halters.

A small gold plate rested on the door of every stall, a different horse's name engraved on each one. A wooden peg to the left of every door held a halter and lead for each horse. As he entered the stable, Aston noticed Talbot at the other end, some poor groom saddling his ride. Shaking his head, Aston started down the hall to Sterling's stall. He stopped to pat his rouncey, Edward, on the nose before continuing to the stall of his courser. He let himself inside and whispered soothing words to the animal as he slipped a red halter over his long silver nose.

The dappled grey beauty was the fastest of all the coursers in Fridel. The horse had been his loyal companion since the beast had been born. Aston had trained Sterling himself, and there was no better mount for a knight. He led Sterling from the stall, taking him to the back wall to be tacked.

Tying Sterling's lead to a waist high wooden bar, the knight went to the tack room to pick out a saddle and bridle before going back to Sterling. He quickly brushed the animal, checking for burs, before settling a wool blanket over the horse's back, topping it with the saddle. He tightened the girth on his saddle, looking up when the animal made an annoyed grunt.

"I know, boy," Aston said, rubbing the horse's neck. "You didn't get much time to rest, and I apologize. Once we are back, I will refuse the next mission in favor of some rest." Seeming satisfied, Sterling turned back around, allowing him to finish.

"Are you ready yet, O mighty warrior?" Talbot asked sarcastically.

Aston mouthed some names he would love to call Talbot before answering. "I'm ready. Are you?"

"Of course." Talbot mounted Red, a glorious red bay that he'd named himself. While the horse could be fast if he had to be, he shared Talbot's demeanor for the most part. Being lazy and impossible were the horse's best qualities.

"Then, we ride." Aston climbed nimbly onto Sterling's back and guided the horse out of his stall, onto the path leading out the palace gates. Talbot followed behind, but Aston didn't check to see how far behind he was. It wouldn't be his fault if the lazy prince got lost. Talbot had always been a good rider; it was the one thing in his life he seemed passionate about. Aston knew he could count on Talbot catching up with him if the prince *did* lag behind.

Fridel's largest city, the one closest to the castle and named after the country's first king, bustled with life as Aston and the prince rode through. People stopped to wave as they passed, and while Talbot chose to ignore everyone, the knight smiled and waved back. He passed a quick smile to Zane, the town jeweler and also a good friend of his. Aston's younger sister, Eiko, met them on the path at the edge of town.

"Ride fast, brother, and return home to us," she told him. Aston climbed down from Sterling to pull his younger sister into a firm hug. Her golden hair whipped into his face in the gentle wind, and her sweet, lavender scent invaded his nose.

"You've been playing in Father's lavender garden again, haven't you?" he scolded. Eiko smiled but didn't answer, instead pulling her brother into a firmer hug. When she pulled away, her light blue eyes were wet with unshed tears.

"Be safe, brother." Aston nodded, giving her a smile before mounting Sterling again.

"Tell Father I will return home soon," he told her. Eiko smiled and ran off, extending her arms as if she were a bird, about to take flight. Aston smiled as he watched her disappear in the crowd flooding Fridel's streets.

"Now can we go? It's hot, just sitting here," Talbot said, a slight whine to his voice. Aston sighed. They hadn't even left Fridel yet and already the prince was anxious. The sun was still high in the sky as they left the town's streets and started down the hard-packed dirt road to Adion. It promised to be a long ride.

"One of the hardest things in life is having words in your heart that you can't utter."

- James Earl Jones -

Two

Jade sighed as her mother pulled her toward the ballroom. Her burgundy dress swirled around her feet as she walked, her auburn curls bouncing against her back.

"Come now, Jade. We don't want to keep them waiting." Queen Margaret continued to stride forward, tugging lightly at her daughter's wrist. The queen's greying hair had been twisted into a tight bun, held in place by various pins, each one shining with gemstones. Her navy dress was much fuller than Jade's, barely moving as her thin frame glided down the hallway.

Jade tried to match her mother's pace, but she still found herself taking two steps to match every one of the queen's. She didn't know what the fuss was about. This ball would be her last outing as an unmarried woman. The next night, her father intended to announce her marriage to Duke Aeron's eldest son, Marquess Jacob of Summerslade. This ball was a final celebration in her mind, though her father had described it as something different.

"One last chance to mingle with your friends," Jade muttered under her breath.

Margaret heard her and looked back at her daughter, her small hazel eyes narrowed. "Watch your tone, young lady. Your father has worked hard to convince Duke Aeron to come to Adion, and even harder to convince him to allow Jacob to marry you."

"Oh, he's *allowing* Jacob to marry me? So Jacob had a choice and I didn't?" Jade asked, pulling her wrist from her mother's grasp and stopping.

The queen sighed and turned to face the princess. "Jade, now is not the time for this.

"Then when, Mother? At the altar, before I am promised to Marquess Jacob? Years from now, when I have born his children? When is the time for this?" Jade asked, exasperated. She wasn't ready to be married. She was nineteen, past the age she should have been married off, but her father had waited this long to pick a suitor. Why couldn't he wait just a bit longer?

"Oh, daughter, *really?* Is this necessary? Jacob is a fine man. He will be good for you."

"I don't want a man that is *good for me,* Mother. I want a man that cares about me and wants to know my thoughts," the princess argued, turning away from the queen and crossing her arms over her chest.

"Well, you won't find a man like that. Women are objects to men, Jade. I don't love your father, but he has done things for me that the boy I loved as a young woman could never have done. So, who is it, Jade? Who is this man that makes you think love is more important than status?"

Jade sighed and closed her eyes. Her mother would never understand. "There is no man, Mother. That's the problem! I have never known love, and with Jacob, I never will!"

"You don't know that. You hardly know the man!"

"One more reason I shouldn't be *marrying* him," she replied, her tone curt. Jade opened her eyes again as her wrist was roughly grabbed. Her mother was staring at her with a sternness she had never shown.

"You are going to marry Marquess Jacob in two days and you are going to enjoy this ball. Your father put this together so you could spend one last night with your friends before you go to Summerslade with Jacob."

"Go to Summerslade? *Leave* Adion? How could I? This is my home!" Jade exclaimed. She tried to pull her hand away again, but her mother's grip was strong.

"It is your duty. Now, come and dance with your cousin. He has waited all night to dance with you and you have been hiding away in your chambers. It is most unbecoming of a lady and a hostess."

They entered the ballroom and Jade forced a smile onto her lips. She could be unhappy with her mother all she wanted, but if she showed that emotion in front of her parents' friends, she would get an earful later. Instead, she would pretend to be happy until their guests retired for the evening.

The du Halen family's ballroom was nothing short of spectacular. Deep mahogany wood floors, gleaming marble pillars and emerald curtains surrounded Jade as she made her way across the room. All around, pairs were dancing. Dresses in all colors swirled around her while men in coats waltzed their partners across the floor.

"Oh, Uri. Thank you so much for coming." She smiled, curtsying to her cousin.

The young man smiled back at her, his dimples showing. "I wouldn't miss it, Jade. Would you care to dance?"

With a slight nod, Jade took her cousin's hand and allowed him to lead her around the floor. They twirled past couples, some of whom Jade knew and others that were unfamiliar to her. They all smiled politely at her as she spun past them, and Jade returned the expressions halfheartedly. She found herself wishing she were still in her room, lying on her bed in her beautiful gown and dreaming of a different life.

She noticed her father across the room. King Aric was speaking in low voices with high ranking officials from three of the countries that bordered them. King Damien of Azazel was there, his face sunken. The death of his son had been hard on the king. The kings from Summerslade and Fridel were absent, but Duke Aeron was there, as well as the prince of Canterbury. His name escaped Jade at the moment. She was more concerned with the worried lines etched into the faces of each man in the circle.

"What are they speaking about?" Jade asked Uri, motioning to her father with her head. She didn't stop dancing; she had to keep up appearances. The smile didn't even slip from her lips.

Uri looked at the circle of men before turning back to Jade, one brow raised. "You haven't heard about the letter?"

Jade shook her head. "What letter?"

"The Rogue Royal has targeted Duke Aeron. He is supposed to strike tonight, at the stroke of midnight. This ball is a huge controversy right now. Many people have said that your father has no class, holding the ball with the duke's life in danger." Uri looked at her apologetically, but Jade waved away his words.

"Why would the Rogue strike here instead of waiting until Aeron is back in Summerslade?"

"Some have said it is a message to King Aric."

"A message about what?" Jade asked, sneaking another quick glance at her father. He was looking at her as well, but he quickly turned away when he met her gaze.

"About you and your marriage to Marquess Jacob. They say it is a warning."

"That's ridiculous." Jade snorted, though she knew the predictions may be right. It sounded like something the Rogue would do. He always did want what was best for her. She wished he would be more discreet. At this rate, he was bound to be caught.

"Maybe, but nevertheless, people are talking."

"Mother says that no talk is bad talk, because even if the gossip is bad, they are still talking about you," Jade announced. She wished she knew more about the night's events, but she couldn't question her father with the other men. They would frown at her and tell her to leave, like she was a child.

Sometimes, she hated being a woman.

"I am prepared to die, but there is no cause for which I am prepared to kill."
- Mahatma Gandhi -

Three

A day's ride and many inconvenient stops later, nighttime found Aston hunched in the forest outside the castle of Adion, Prince Talbot at his side. They were hidden behind a thin group of cypress trees in view of the palace gates. No one had entered yet, and Aston wondered if they'd gotten the day and time wrong. He found himself wishing King Donn had told King Aric of their arrival, but, as usual, the king hadn't burdened himself with the pleasantries.

Instead, he had Talbot and Aston standing guard outside the palace walls, too far away to be of any help if the Rogue *did* appear.

"Why is it so damn cold in August?" Talbot asked, pulling his blanket tighter around himself and glaring at Aston. Talbot had requested a fire, but the knight had refused. A fire would draw attention to their position, and they needed the secrecy.

"It's a few hours to midnight, Sire. It's windy and close to fall. It's bound to be cold. You just aren't used to being outside after dark," Aston answered. He knew he was being overly snooty to the prince, but he was tired of Talbot's whining. He'd had to listen to him complain about being sore for the majority of the ride, and Talbot hadn't helped at all with making camp. Or dinner. So now, Aston was happy to see him suffer.

"Well, what's taking so long! The Rogue should have shown up and killed someone already."

"Prince Talbot, the point is to *not* let him kill anyone, not to wish for someone to die faster," he scolded the prince.

"Fine. Wake me up when it's time to actually *do* something." The prince pulled his blanket over his head and lay down, pulling his feet under the cover. Aston sent a prayer to Heaven, thanking his Lord for finally making Talbot sleep. He'd hear about his attitude later from King Donn, but for now he was happy to let the prince wallow in his misery.

As the hours passed, Aston found himself taking in his surroundings. In front of him, the great stone wall that surrounded Adion's palace towered, slowly turning green as rogue moss took over. A narrow, dirt road led from the castle to the actual city, where no light could be found. Everyone lay in bed, sleeping. Aston snuck a glance at Talbot, grimacing as a loud snore ripped through the prince's open mouth. *So much for being subtle.* Once again, Aston found himself wishing King Donn had sent an experienced soldier with him instead of the prince.

Another hour passed before anything happened. Aston looked up at the wall surrounding the castle and saw a light flash once, followed by two short flashes and then a long third one.

Something was wrong. Someone was signaling for help. His heart racing, Aston shook the prince, pushing his shoulder as hard as he could until he heard Talbot murmur.

"Wake up, Sire. We need to get in there," he said. With one final shove, he stood and crept toward the wall, keeping low to the ground. He didn't know if Talbot was following him or not, but he wasn't stopping to check. The knight had a feeling the Rogue resided somewhere in the palace, heading for his target. While he would have loved to leave Talbot behind, he couldn't let anything happen to the prince.

Aston took his grappling hook from his belt, swinging it in a wide circle beside his body as he neared the wall. With one well-practiced throw, the hook caught. A quick look over his shoulder showed him that Talbot was slowly following him. Using the strength in his arms and very careful steps, Aston made it over the wall fairly quickly, despite the moss that kept trying to make him lose his footing. Once over, he dropped to the thin, wooden walkway on the other side. The guard that had been positioned there was dead, his throat slit. Whatever danger he had seen had already left, undoubtedly the murderer.

"Dammit." Aston leaned over the wall. The prince was two thirds of the way up, moving sluggishly, struggling to find his footing. "Prince Talbot! I'm going ahead. Stay close, and hurry! We don't know how far ahead of us the Rogue is," he shouted, knowing no one was around to hear him. He ran along the walkway until he got to a set of stairs, taking them three at a time to get into the palace. He heard the prince clomping along behind him.

All the torches were snuffed out in the hallway he entered. Aston stopped and listened, trying to locate people, but he couldn't hear anything. It was late, but there should have been guards patrolling every inch of the palace. The duke's life had been threatened.

He could feel his throat constricting as he crept close to the wall and started down the hallway, more alert now than he had been before. This wasn't his first mission, but it was the first time he'd been ordered to save a man's life. Normally, he was sent to battles or as a messenger. This mission had a completely different feel, and something deep inside told him he was already too late.

The wide corridor forked off in two directions at the end. The left side was dark, the right lit. Aston headed left, knowing The Rogue Royal would be somewhere in the darkened corridors. He paused at the end of the second hallway, listening again. Something rammed into his back and he turned quickly, pulling a dagger from his belt and crouching down.

"Don't kill me, Rogue, please!" Talbot screamed. He looked up from the ground where he'd fallen, slightly dazed. Aston sighed and put his dagger away, quickly shushing Talbot.

"Sire, please! You'll give away our position. I told you to stay close," he snapped in a harsh whisper, turning back around without offering his prince a hand. He felt Talbot at his back but ignored him, listening intently for the sound of footsteps.

A scream ripped through the silent corridor, a woman crying out for help. Immediately, Talbot went from terrified to courageous. He ran off in the direction of the scream, likely intending to be a hero.

"Talbot, dammit, come back!" Aston stage whispered. The prince did not listen, and Aston took off after him, drawing his sword in case they met the Rogue on the way. Maybe King Donn had been wrong. Maybe the Rogue had targeted the princess, or the queen.

Talbot entered a room on their left about twenty feet ahead of Aston just as another figure exited the room across the hall. As the man saw Aston, he turned and ran. The clock on the wall began its twelve chimes as Aston left Talbot to tend to the woman, running after the man racing down the corridor. He jumped over the bodies of dead knights as he chased the Rogue, not glancing down at them for fear of recognizing someone. He couldn't afford to stop.

The Rogue made it to another room, and when Aston entered it, he cursed. Four doors led off in different directions from the room, each one a possible escape route for the murderer. Aston opened each door, listening for running footsteps. Each dark hallway was quiet. There was no way he would catch the murderer now.

Disappointed, Aston retraced his steps, heading back toward Talbot, carefully stepping over each fallen guard. The men's armor was bloodstained, their throats slit open. Aston grimaced as his boot slipped in a small puddle of ruby liquid. He kept his eyes ahead of him then, not thinking about the corpses. While he'd killed many men in his years as a knight, he'd never murdered anyone in cold blood or without orders to.

When he finally reached the hall where he'd left his prince, a crowd had gathered, Talbot standing at its center. His shoulders were back, his neck extended in a regal manner as he addressed the crowd. "We were sent to catch The Rogue Royal by King Donn. I am Prince Talbot of Fridel. This is Aston Smith, Knight of Fridel," Talbot said, motioning to Aston. The knight nodded at the faces that turned toward him, but they quickly looked back at Talbot. "We received word that the Duke of Northsbury would be visiting and that The Rogue Royal would be attempting to murder him."

"He did not attempt," a woman said, slowly walking toward them. Aston recognized her as Duchess Viola, the Duke's wife. Her eyes were red rimmed, dripping with tears, her greying hair stuck to her face. She was wearing a thin white gown and her feet were concealed beneath pale pink slippers. She held a handkerchief to her mouth as she wept. "He succeeded. My husband is dead." The woman broke down again and a chambermaid came to her, walking her into another room.

King Aric appeared at the end of the hallway, which was now flooded with light. His auburn beard was too long and his face looked older than it should. His blue satin long-johns would have been comical had the situation been different. He stopped by Aston, placing a hand on the knight's shoulder before making his way through the crowd and into the room where Duke Aeron had spent his last moments.

Aston sighed and turned away, not wanting to see Duke Aeron in death. He could picture the man in his mind, the Duke's eyes open, burgundy blood blossoming from his chest. He placed a hand on Talbot's elbow and motioned in the opposite direction with his head. Talbot nodded and plodded after Aston as they left the palace, their mission failed. The Duke had passed and The Rogue Royal had escaped.

King Donn would not be pleased.

"What was any art but a mould in which to imprison for a moment the shining elusive element which is life itself - life hurrying past us and running away, too strong to stop, too sweet to lose."

- Willa Sibert Cather -

Four

"It's hot today," Talbot announced. Aston glanced sideways at the prince, but otherwise remained quiet. "Don't you think it's hot?" Again, the knight didn't answer. Talbot huffed and slouched in his saddle.

Aston had no desire to speak to the prince. Duke Aeron could have easily been saved, had Talbot not been so worried about a prospective damsel in distress. If he had turned right instead of left, they would be going home as honorable men; heroes, even. Instead, they would return to Fridel bearing bad news. The knight turned his head to the right, staring at the vast countryside that made up Adion. It was amazing how different the two kingdoms were. Fridel was made up of mostly forest while Adion was open land with hardly any trees.

"Did you see that deer?" Talbot asked, pointing off in the distance. Again, Aston ignored him, instead turning to face the road. "Aston Smith, I order you to speak to me."

Aston pulled Sterling up short and turned in his saddle, glaring at the prince. "Sire, with all due respect, I have no desire to speak with you right now. I'm a little busy trying to decide how we are going to inform His Majesty of Duke Aeron's death," he spat.

Talbot appeared taken aback by his comment, but his face quickly turned angry. "You can go to your chambers when we reach Fridel. *I* will deal with my father."

Aston nodded and started forward again. He wasn't sure if letting the prince do the talking was a good idea, but he was more than happy to let him take the brunt of the king's anger.

The rest of the ride passed in silence, and when they again reached Fridel, Aston went to his chambers, as ordered. He plopped down on his bed, throwing his satchel across the room. King Donn wouldn't understand what had happened. He would question Talbot, but not Aston. The knight pondered what would happen to the two of them. If Donn had trained Talbot to fight, as princes normally were, instead of letting him do what he wanted for the past twenty years, then maybe Talbot wouldn't be in his current position; and neither would Aston

**

Talbot went straight to the throne room, where he knew his father would be expecting a report. He'd watched until Aston descended the stairs to the knights' quarters before going to his father. Once there, the prince motioned to the guards to shut the doors with an order to not let anyone in before striding down the carpet to the king.

The prince stood at the foot of the throne instead of taking his place next to his father. After Aston's comment, he'd spent the day's ride thinking of a way to pin the failure on the knight. His father was a very unforgiving man, and Talbot didn't want to face the king's wrath so soon after his last mistake in Canterbury. Though Aston was the best knight, this mission proved that he wasn't perfect. Talbot himself was irreplaceable, so Aston would take the fall for the mission and the prince would be spared. King

Donn would never understand his desire to save the distressed woman over saving Duke Aeron.

"Father, we return," he started. King Donn nodded, waiting for his son to continue. "I am sorry to say that the Rogue Royal managed to escape." Talbot had the decency to appear saddened by his news, though truthfully, he didn't care. He hadn't liked the duke much and didn't feel it was such a big loss. However, he knew his father had respected the man, and his thoughts would be different.

"What happened, Talbot? How could you let this happen?" His father's voice dominated the throne room, ricocheting off columns and echoing in the space between the floor and the high ceilings. Talbot flinched, but didn't look away from his father's slowly reddening face as the king stood. He towered over the prince, and Talbot fought not to lose his resolve.

"It was Aston's fault, Father. The palace at Adion went silent so we crept inside, keeping close to the walls and dodging patches of light. We were halfway down a darkened corridor when we heard a woman scream and Aston left his position, taking off toward the woman's voice. I followed after him and he entered the maiden's room to make sure she was alright. Meanwhile, the Rogue Royal came from the room behind us.

"He could have killed me, Father! I drew my sword and we fought for a moment in the corridor. Then Aston came out of the room and drew his sword, but the Rogue knew he could not fight us both, so he ran. I followed, but lost him in the maze of the unfamiliar palace. Aston stayed behind to help the woman. We could have stopped him, Father, but we were too late. Aston's foolish behavior caused Duke Aeron to be killed." Talbot hung his head in mock shame and shook his head.

"You're sure that's what happened, Talbot?" the king asked, narrowing his eyes at his son.

Talbot swallowed thickly before answering. "Of course, Father? Why would I lie?"

After one last appraisal of his son, the king abruptly left the room. Talbot smiled, knowing what would happen. Aston would be charged with treason and hanged. The knowledge that it had been his fault the Duke was killed would die with the knight.

**

Aston stood from his bed when King Donn charged in, his face livid.

"You, Sir, are a disgrace to the title knight! Leaving a criminal loose in the palace to save a woman! Duke Aeron was a kind man and one of my closest friends. Your mission was to save *Duke Aeron*, not to gallivant around with the castle's women. I will see you hanged for this, Aston Smith, I guarantee it," the king said, pointing an accusing finger at the knight.

Aston stood with his mouth open, gaping at the king for a moment before speaking. "With all due respect, your Majesty, what are you talking about?"

Donn's anger flared, his face turning an even deeper shade of scarlet. "Don't play daft with me, Sir! Talbot told me everything!"

That explains it, Aston thought. "Sire, I can explain," he began, but King Donn cut him off.

"I don't want to hear a word from you, Aston Smith! I want you arrested and thrown in the dungeon!"

"But Sire--"

"I should have listened to Talbot when he told me to send another knight. I was foolish, thinking you could handle this. I…"

"Your Majesty!" This time Aston yelled, causing the king to stop his babbling and look at his knight. King Donn's eyes were wide with shock.

"Your Majesty," Aston said, quieter now, "Prince Talbot lied to you. He is the one who gave away our position, as well as the one who went for the woman instead of checking on Duke Aeron. I understand he was a friend of yours, and I apologize, but you should be yelling at your son, *not* me." Aston had hoped his words would calm the king's fury enough to make him listen to reason, but he only made the king angrier.

"Talbot? You accuse my *son*? Do you really think your lies will save your life? Talbot loved Duke Aeron like a second father! He would never throw away duty for a woman!"

Aston grimaced. It seemed King Donn was one more person that Talbot had fooled. It hadn't hurt to try. Either way, his sentence would be the same. There was no dishonor in trying to make the king see reason, even though his rights allowed him a trial.

"Guards! Guards! Come now and arrest this traitor!" At King Donn's beckoning, four soldiers rushed into the room, swords drawn.

Aston slowly backed away, nearing his window. He didn't have time to think. In one swift movement, he grabbed his still-packed bag from the floor, pulled his grappling hook from his belt, and leapt from the window, praying the hook would catch.

He almost took a relieved breath when the metal claw caught on the window and he was safely on the ground, his knees taking the blunt of the blow. But he was still in danger; he couldn't stop yet. He dropped his rope and ran, cringing as the palace bells sounded behind him. He ran as fast as he could toward the stable, reaching them just as Vernon was about to remove Sterling's bridle. The old man looked up in surprise when Aston came charging in, but didn't stop him from jumping on Sterling's back, grabbing a halter from the wall, and riding out of the stable at top speed.

Aston raced into the night, reaching the drawbridge just as it was being closed and jumping his horse across the river. The sound of hooves pounding the hard earth behind him had Aston driving Sterling faster, digging his heels into the animal's side as his own heart raced with adrenaline. An arrow embedded itself in a tree to his right and he ducked out of instinct. Looking behind him, he saw a man with a bow guiding his horse with his knees, notching another arrow.

Aston cursed, leaning low in Sterling's saddle and running the horse in a zigzag along the forest's edge. With a curse, he made Sterling take a fast right, plunging the horse into the thick brush and crashing through low hanging tree branches. He heard men hollering from behind him, upset that they'd lost him in the forest. A couple of brave soldiers followed, but Aston wasn't too worried about them. These woods took up almost half of Fridel, and he'd grown up in them. They wouldn't be able to find him now.

Regardless, he kept their current pace until he could no longer hear the angry voices of knights calling for him. Sterling's withers were slick with foam and sweat before he finally slowed the laboring creature. His own heart had settled once he'd realized he wasn't being followed, and now he allowed his horse to rest, taking up a slower pace. He dropped down from the saddle and walked, allowing Sterling to cool off from his run.

"A traitor, Sterling. He called me a traitor," he said, patting his horse on the neck. His mind couldn't wrap around the idea. He had been King Donn's best knight, had never failed a mission. Now he was a traitor? Because of a lie Talbot had told?

He found a place where the trees were thin and climbed off of Sterling, petting the animal and whispering soothing words to him as he tied the horse to a thick branch by his halter, allowing him room to bend and graze if he wished. A small stream nearby offered water for a cool bath and drinking, which Aston gladly partook of. The gently flowing water made light, tinkling sounds as it wound around small boulders. Different colored fish jumped every few feet, gleaming in the slim beams of moonlight drifting through the forest's roof.

Once undressed, Aston stepped into the cool, waist-deep, water. He sighed as the dirt decorating his skin was erased, leaving him feeling fresh and unhindered. His worries washed away with the current and he lay back, floating softly on top of the water for a moment before setting his feet on the stream's floor again.

Aston didn't know how much time he spent in the water. When he stepped from the cool, refreshing stream, his finger tips were pruned, soft and wrinkled, but he felt better. He felt like he could think again. He dressed, shaking his clothes to rid them of some of the dirt they were covered in, before going back to his horse. The knight untied Sterling and brought him to the stream, allowing him to drink while his master thought.

As Sterling pawed at the cool water and took big, gulping drinks, Aston tried to think of a place to go. He needed somewhere to rest until he knew what to do. He never should have run from the palace, but he wasn't ready to die. Something had taken him over, made him run when his future started to disappear. Suddenly, he knew where he needed to go, at least until he figured everything out. Aston mounted and turned Sterling south, heading towards the one place he knew he would always feel safe.

"A friend is someone who understands your past, believes in your future, and accepts you just the way you are."
- Abraham Lincoln -

Five

Aston sighed in relief as the little wood cabin slowly materialized from behind the trees. It had taken him all night and half the morning to reach it, and now, with it so close, he just wanted to be there already. He sped Sterling into a gallop, racing toward a place where he knew there would be a soft, warm bed and a hot meal waiting for him.

As he got closer and the trees thinned, he could make out the sound of an axe meeting wood. His nose picked up sweet aromas coming from the chimney, a mixture of cinnamon, apple, and the sweet, thick smell of smoke coming from a brick oven. Once he was within shouting distance, Aston let Sterling slow and took in all that surrounded him.

The cabin sat in an almost perfect circle of trees, some of them no more than stumps sticking up from the hard ground. The trees cast the cabin mostly in shadow, though there were some places the sun was still able to reach. It had two windows on the front and one on the back; this he knew by heart. The door had a half moon cut out of it, filled in with glass and the roof was covered in pine needles, giving it an orange look to accent the brown logs of its sides. Aston grinned as he got closer and saw his friend, Delgrab, outside. The man took one last swing at the tree he was demolishing and looked up, his sweaty brow crinkling as he grinned at Aston. "Well, hello, old friend. It's been a long time."

Aston dismounted Sterling and strode to Delgrab, meeting the tall, burly man in a firm hug. He nodded at Delgrab's words and felt suddenly at peace. It had been too long since he'd been away from the palace and his duties as a knight. Even though he wasn't truly away now, he still felt like he could relax. This place always did that to him.

"Aye, it has been. I apologize for that. Something smells amazing." Aston was never shy here. He was welcome anytime. Delgrab's wife, Alys, always made sure of that.

Aston wasn't sure how someone as rough around the edges as Delgrab had managed to attract Alys. She was the most beautiful woman he had ever seen, and he spent most of his time around royalty, the primped and perfect. She was a woman who did not fit the norm for beauty; Alys was plump and short, with blonde hair that cascaded in waves down her back and striking hazel eyes with just a hint of gold. She was a motherly woman; she took care of anyone and anything that walked through her door. Just thinking about Alys made Aston want to go into the house and see her; he'd missed her warm smile and her amazing cooking.

"Well, of course it does! My Alys is the greatest cook in the country! Go on in! I'm going to finish up here and then head inside. Don't start without me." Delgrab turned back to his work as Aston took Sterling around to the stables behind the cabin.

He'd spent most of his youth out here with Delgrab. It had been Delgrab's father's cabin back then. They'd used to run and play and pretend to be knights, hunting dragons in the surrounding forest and rescuing damsels daily. Aston had always bragged about how he would be a real knight one day.

"Look at me now. Some knight," Aston muttered. He sighed again, suddenly not feeling as relaxed, and headed back toward the house once Sterling was settled.

As soon as he entered the cabin, his shoulder muscles loosened and his mind felt suddenly at ease. Though it was not quite fall and still a bit warm outside, Alys had a fire going. It kept the room warm, but not stuffy. Another fire was lit in a brick oven in the kitchen area. That's where Aston found Alys. She was bent over the stove, stirring something in a big black cauldron, when Aston walked into the room.

"I hope you washed your hands before you came in here," Alys stated. She turned around, likely to scold Delgrab. Her eyes widened and her face broke out in a beautiful white toothed smile when she saw Aston. "Oh, Aston! Delgrab didn't tell me you were coming!" she exclaimed, wiping her hands on her apron and rushing to give him a hug. He picked her up in his arms and swung her around once before depositing her back on the floor.

"He didn't know, if that helps him any. I wasn't planning on visiting. I just sort of… arrived," he said, hoping his being there wouldn't be too much of an inconvenience. He needn't have worried. Alys was one of those women who were always prepared, no matter what life threw at her. She reassured Aston that she had a room he could stay in and plenty of clean sheets. She told him not to worry about a thing and to go and wash up for dinner. With another smile, Aston nodded at the woman before heading into the back. When he turned around to look back at her, Alys was already setting another place at the table.

Shaking his head, Aston closed himself in the small bath area. A tub sat at the far end of the room, logs set up underneath to warm the water. There was a small wooden table with a basin on it in front of a tall mirror hanging on the wall. A pitcher full of water sat beside the basin and Aston poured some of the water into the bowl. Less than two days on the road and already he felt dirtier than he had in his life.

The knight had spent plenty of time outdoors. He'd spent weeks out on missions before, but this felt different. Maybe because he was running. It was his soul that was dirty, not his skin. Aston quickly washed his face and hands, wanting to get back to his friends as soon as he could. He'd had enough with the depressing thoughts for the night.

In the kitchen, Alys was putting the finishing touches on a homegrown salad. Delgrab was already at the table, chugging a huge goblet of water. Aston took a long look at his friend, noticing the subtle changes in the man. His dark beard was starting to turn grey and had grown well past the man's chin. Brown eyes were starting to wrinkle around the edges from hard times, but his mouth was forever curled up in a smile. His pants were snugger than they had been before, and Aston thought that without the suspenders, his friend's pants would snap right off. His white shirt was covered in dirt and drenched in sweat, and his boots were covered in mud. Alys was eyeing them, but Delgrab paid her no mind.

The man spent his days outside, chopping trees and building wooden furniture. When he came in for the night, he did everything he could to make sure his wife was happy while playfully teasing her. If ever Aston needed a place to stay, he was always willing to help. Delgrab was the most selfless person the knight had met in his life, nothing like the monarchs he was used to.

Aston took his spot at the table as Alys brought the last of the food out, and the three settled into a comfortable routine.

"So, how's life at the palace, Aston?" Alys asked. She was always too insightful for her own good. She was only asking because she knew something was wrong.

"It's great, Alys. Just taking a little break," he lied. He didn't have the heart to worry the woman.

"Alys has been trying to perfect her apple pie recipe lately," Delgrab interjected, and Aston was grateful for the change of subject. Alys sent him a pointed glare, but Delgrab glared right back

"Perfect it? I didn't know anything was wrong with it," Aston answered, turning his attention from his plate to Alys. She smiled and blushed, looking down. He tried to ignore the tension his unannounced arrival had caused.

"Oh, stop it, boys. You just know I've got one in the oven now and you want some," she said. Aston and Delgrab both laughed as Alys stood and took her pie from the oven, setting it on a raised wooden rack to cool before retaking her spot at the table. The rest of the conversation was light, and Aston was grateful his reason for visiting didn't come up again.

When dinner and dessert were done and the dishes were put away, Alys excused herself for a bath. Delgrab motioned for Aston to sit on the couch in the living area, which he did so reluctantly. He knew what was coming. As Delgrab sat beside him, Aston looked everywhere but at his friend. Instead, he focused on his surroundings, letting his eyes wander around the familiar cabin.

Not much had changed since the last time he'd been there. The curtains over the windows were the same dark hunter green ones that Alys had made years ago. The sofa was made of thick logs that Delgrab had strung together and carved out, making a seat that curved inwards. Alys had sewn two green cushions to fit perfectly into the curve, making a soft surface to rest on. The small end tables beside the piece matched. Most of the floor was hidden underneath various animal skin rugs, prizes of Delgrab's hunts, and a couple of deer "trophies" adorned the space over the hearth.

As his gaze neared the end of the room Aston finally made his eyes meet Delgrab's. His friend was looking at him expectantly, waiting for him to tell his story. Aston realized Delgrab wouldn't leave him alone until he knew exactly why, after three years of planned meetings, the knight would suddenly turn up unannounced.

"I'm in trouble, Del," he began. Delgrab's eyes widened a bit, but otherwise he didn't react. Taking that as a sign to continue, Aston moved on. "I was sent on a mission with Prince Talbot. You know who the Rogue Royal is?" At this, Delgrab nodded. "King Donn received word from King Aric that the Rogue was going to kill Duke Aeron. Donn sent Talbot and I to stop him, but Talbot messed up. We were supposed to wait outside and catch him as he was leaving, but everything was so still that Talbot and I went inside. Everything was fine until a woman screamed and Talbot ran off. The Rogue managed to kill his target and escaped. Talbot blamed everything on me and now…" Aston stopped, not sure how much he wanted to give away.

"Now you're on the run because you basically abandoned all of your duties to come here," Delgrab finished for him. Aston shook his head.

"I didn't mean to come here. I shouldn't have come here at all. I'm putting you and Alys at risk. I apologize for that. I didn't know where else to go. Do you know what the punishment is for killing a monarch, for killing anyone you aren't told to kill? Death, Delgrab. They were going to kill me, even though I didn't kill the Duke with my own hands. According to Talbot's story, he would still be alive if I hadn't risked everything to save a woman. I didn't want to die. I don't..." Aston stopped talking as his voice cracked.

He hadn't realized it before now, but he was scared. His situation was finally sinking in. He could never be a knight again. If he ever went back to Fridel, he would be killed. He could never go home, see his father, his baby sister. He would be an outcast wherever he went. Aston felt his throat constrict as his heart started to beat furiously within him. He was having a hard time catching a breath, and his mind raced as he realized all that he had lost.

A hand on his shoulder made him turn to his friend.

"Calm down, Aston. You came to the right place. Don't worry about Alys or me. We can take care of ourselves. What we need to be worried about is how we are going to keep *you* safe." Aston nodded, appreciating his friend's words, but he knew he couldn't stay. He would never forgive himself if something happened to either of them.

"You're right. I'm sorry. Can we talk about this in the morning? I haven't gotten much sleep the past couple of days." Delgrab nodded, and Aston stood. When Delgrab stood as well, Aston pulled the man into another hug. He didn't know when he would see his friend again.

"Well, goodnight," he said, releasing Delgrab and heading to the room Alys had pointed out to him.

"Aston." He stopped and turned back to Delgrab. "Stay tonight, okay? We can talk in the morning."

Aston faked a smile and nodded. Delgrab knew him too well. He knew Aston intended to leave as soon as he and Alys were sleeping. Aston's fake reassurance wouldn't make the man rest any easier, but at least he tried.

Aston lay down and slept, his internal clock waking him four hours later. He rolled over sleepily and debated whether he should really stay until the morning, get a good night's rest, and leave early. He knew he couldn't. As soon as they searched his father's house, Delgrab's cabin would be next. King Donn required his soldiers to map every place they frequented, in case a mission ever came up while they were gone. King Donn liked to know where his knights were at all times.

Aston had to be gone when they came here.

With a curse, he rolled off the bed, immediately missing its warmth and softness, and forced himself to tug on his boots and head outside. The early morning air was cool on his skin and Aston breathed deeply, loving the pine smell. He would miss this place. It had been his second home for the longest time, and now he feared he would never be able to return.

Sterling wasn't pleased being woken in the middle of the night, but the animal cooperated with Aston, and for that he was grateful. He quickly put the horse's bridle back on before saddling him. He swung his satchel over the saddle and then climbed up himself, riding Sterling out of the stable and into the night. He took one last look at the cabin before looking ahead of him and promising never to look back again.

"When small men begin to cast big shadows, it means that the sun is about to set."
- Lyn Yutang –

Six

Early the next morning, Aston took a long drink from the stream he'd stopped at and looked up at the sky. The sun was burning hot as fall slowly became winter, the scorching rays singeing his neck as it tried to survive the season's change. He splashed some water on his neck to cool its burning before climbing back onto Sterling and taking off again.

He wasn't sure where he was going. He knew he had to find a safe place to hide, for a month, at least. He'd planned on staying with Delgrab, but had immediately decided that would bring too much danger to his friend. Instead, he found himself riding through the forest, hoping to come across another cabin. He needed to find someone who rarely visited town, someone like Delgrab, but without the emotional connections. Someone who wouldn't recognize him and immediately run to turn him in, or know who he was at all. As long as it was a place King Donn's soldiers would never look, it would suit him just fine.

Aston stopped Sterling as the bushes next to him rustled. He drew his dagger from his belt and carefully lowered himself from the horse's back. He crouched next to the horse, waiting to see what was causing the ruckus. A small rabbit, solid white with red eyes, emerged from the shrubbery, twitching its nose in Aston's direction. Aston made sure to hold completely still so the animal wouldn't see him as a threat. When the rabbit inched a little closer, Aston pounced, skillfully skewering the small creature on his dagger. The rabbit barely had time to squeal before the life left his eyes.

The knight looked away, saying a small prayer for the creature before picking him up by the feet and tying him to Sterling's saddle. He'd always disliked this part of the job. Aston usually let the other knights travelling with him do the hunting. He didn't like taking lives, of humans *or* animals. Why he'd gone into a profession that required him to do both, he wasn't sure. He liked saving people, but the job almost always came with the opposite end as well.

"Come on, boy," he said to Sterling, climbing back on. "Let's find somewhere to rest for a bit and cook." Urging his horse on, he continued through the trees. He found a quiet clearing and used twigs and flint to create a fire before setting to work skinning his catch. Once the rabbit was cooking, he laid back, pulling a blanket from his satchel and leaning against a tree to rest.

Aston was exhausted. Two days of running and already he wished he could be back at the palace, getting ready for a mission or teaching Richard how to read. The boy would be heartbroken when he heard Aston's story. He'd be forever scarred knowing his mentor had been accused of allowing Duke Aeron to die, of being sentenced to hang and instead running in fear. The brave Aston Smith, reduced to a rodent, living off the forest and hiding in the shadows.

He stood and began to pace, his mind wandering. He wished there was a way for him to get word to Richie, to let the boy know what had *really* happened. It wouldn't be a bad idea to have eyes inside the palace, either, watching Talbot and King Donn to see what happened next. Aston stopped pacing and went back to his rabbit, turning it once before resuming his pace. If

Richie knew what had really happened, he would be more than happy to help. The knight was sure of that. All he needed was a way to meet the boy and give him a message.

As Aston ate his meal minutes later, he thought of the perfect plan. Every few days, Richie went with Madam Louise to the market to fetch cleaning supplies and sometimes extra ingredients for the cooks. If Aston could get Richie alone on their next run, he could tell the boy what had happened. Satisfied, Aston finished his rabbit and packed up again, turning Sterling around and heading back toward Fridel. He needed to find the perfect rendezvous point.

At nightfall he found a quiet niche right outside the city's borders and made camp, foregoing a fire in favor of an extra blanket. If someone saw the smoke and came to investigate, his mission would be a failure. Aston knew what he had to do. Even though The Rogue Royal was the reason he was running in the first place, he knew the man would be the one to clear his name. If the Rogue had seen him at all, he could clarify that Aston had been the one chasing him, not Talbot. Even if The Rogue didn't come clean, at least Aston would know he'd finally caught the man responsible for ending his life as a knight.

As he fell asleep, he dreaded the next day. What he was going to do could ruin everything. If he was spotted, it would be over and he would be hanged. Richie would be watching, probably cheering with the rest of the masses, screaming his name and demeaning words as his life was forced from his throat.

With a shiver Aston jolted awake, images of himself hanging from the gallows still lingering in his mind. A dream. It had only been a dream. Everything had been so vivid; the choking sensation as the rope tightened around his throat, the burn of the ropes on his wrists as he fought to free his hands. Even the look on

Richie's face, the immense hatred he had thought never to see from the boy, was ingrained in his memory.

Aston looked at the sky, slowing lightening from its dark blue to the purple and red hints of dawn. He stood and stretched, his shoulders popping as he pushed his arms above his head. He rolled his neck, listening to it crack, before feeding Sterling an apple and making his way toward town. It was now or never, and he didn't want to give himself time to think about how foolish his idea really was.

**

Madam Louise had always been an early riser; she was training Richard to be the same. She'd taken the boy under her wing when he had failed in the stables working under Master Vernon. The man was cruel and often took a whip to the boy when he wasn't strong enough. Madam Louise had taken pity on Richard and had begged King Donn to put the boy into her care. Though the king wasn't known as being the most benevolent man, he relented.

She'd pulled Richie out of bed early that morning, and now he was struggling to pull his shirt over his head as he yawned, his tired eyes still half closed. Madam Louise helped the boy, patting the shirt down to get rid of lingering wrinkles before leaving the room, instructing Richie to follow.

"Now, Richard, I know how you like to wander. I want you to stay close to me today. That rogue knight is still out there somewhere and I don't want you to get into any trouble, understood?"

"Yes ma'am." The answer was automatic to Richie. He didn't believe Aston was guilty anymore than he believed the sky was green. Aston was the most kind-hearted and truthful man he knew. The knight would never allow a man to be killed simply to save a woman.

Richie sighed and followed after Madam Louise. The woman was stocky and short, but she moved fast and Richie found himself taking three steps to her one. She took good care of him, but he feared she didn't think much of him as a person. He was scrawny for his age, underfed and overworked far too long to really gain any muscle structure. His clothes hung on his thin frame and his hair was scraggly and unkempt. Madam Louise did all she could for him, but only Aston truly valued him.

As they reached the castle walls and were let into the city, Richie felt an odd sensation pass over him. He turned around to face the castle, but the guards were already resealing the gate. No one spared him another glance as he crept away from Madam Louise's side and followed the path he and Aston had worn into the forest on their adventures together.

Aston had always been the closest Richie had to a friend. Aston taught him to read and write, to spell and fight with a dagger. The man had been almost a father to Richie, and one day Aston had snuck him from the castle on Sterling's back and brought the boy to the forest to teach him to ride.

After seeing how much Richie enjoyed being on a horse, it became routine for them. When the knight returned from a mission, he would rest for a couple of days and then bring Richie to the same place to ride Sterling. They'd been so many times in the past three years that the path had been worn down to dirt, no grass daring to grow over their special place.

Richie's heart was pounding as he neared the clearing. He had a feeling inside of him that was unfamiliar. Fear? No, that wasn't it. Anger? No. Excitement; that's what it was. He was anticipating what was about to happen. He knew it would be something amazing; surely this feeling bubbling through him couldn't be a lie.

As Richie stepped into the clearing, his heart skipped a beat and his breath caught in his throat. Aston was there, sitting in the center of the clearing on a stump. He smiled as Richie drew near, and the boy mimicked the expression.

"Richie, I have to tell you something," Aston began, but the boy raced toward him and threw his arms around Aston's waist and the words caught in his throat.

"I was so worried about you, Sir Aston! I just knew they would find you and hurt you!" Richie cried, tears slowly falling from his eyes.

"You don't have to worry, Richie. I'm fine. I am going to find the man responsible for this and then everything will be okay again. I will teach you to write and you will be a fine man someday," Aston promised. "Right now, though, I need you to listen to me, okay? This is very important, Richie."

Richie looked up at him and nodded, excited. Aston had always said he would take Richie on a grand adventure, away from Fridel, someday when he was older. The boy had a feeling that adventure was about to happen.

"Talbot and I were sent to find The Rogue Royal, but something went terribly wrong. Prince Talbot messed up the mission, and The Rogue got away. Now, don't you dare say anything to anyone about this. You can't tell Prince Talbot, King Donn, or even Madam Louise, okay? I don't want you getting hurt. Do you understand?" Again, Richie nodded, desperate to hear more. "Good. Now, what I want you to do is keep an eye on Talbot. See if the king gets any more messages from other monarchs about the Rogue Royal. If you get word, come find me here on the full moon. Do you understand?"

"Oh, yes, Sir! I will be the best spy ever!" Richie exclaimed.

"Don't be spotted. Don't let anyone know what you are doing. I don't care what happens to me, but I won't let anything happen to you, do you understand?"

"Yes, Sir Aston. I understand." Richie smiled, bouncing lightly on his feet. He was going to be a real spy. He was going to get to help Aston, and he'd been right all along about the knight being innocent. Of course he'd been right. He'd known all along.

"Good. Now, run along and find Madam Louise. Tell her your shoe came untied and you fell behind. Remember, you never saw me here." Richie saluted and laughed, giving Aston one last hug before skipping off into the trees, humming lightly as he left Aston hidden in the forest behind him.

*"Life can either be accepted or changed.
If it is not accepted, it must be changed.
If it cannot be changed, then it must be accepted."*
- Unknown Author -

Seven

Jade scowled at the woman staring back at her from her mirror. The woman was beautiful with her auburn hair curling to her thin hips, emerald eyes shining in the morning sun, and a diamond tiara sitting atop her head. The dress she wore was elegant, all white lace and corseted middle. She looked fit to rule, and her father planned on giving her away that evening.

Cringing at the thought, Jade turned, struggling to breathe in the too-tight dress. If there was one thing she disliked about being a princess, it was always having to look her best. If she was in a bad mood, tired, or just generally lazy, no one cared; she still had to act like each day was a gift. As she made her way across the room, Jade reached behind her and started pulling on the corsets bottom laces, loosening it enough to allow her lungs to expand. She took a huge gulp of air before turning around and falling backwards onto her bed.

The ball the night before had lasted until eleven. At that time, everyone had retired to their rooms for the night. The Rogue had come at midnight and taken Duke Aeron's life, but still her father wanted the marriage to continue. Now that his father was gone, Jacob was being rushed to the palace; they were to be wed immediately. She grimaced, thinking about the man she was to marry. Jacob was just entering his twentieth year but still acted like a child. He was conceited and needy; Jade wanted nothing to do with the man.

"It isn't fair, Kira," she told her fluffy tawny feline. The cat had jumped onto her bed when Jade had collapsed and now sat curled by her side. The cat purred in agreement, rubbing her head along Jade's arm, begging for affection. The princess gave in, petting her beautiful feline before standing and calling for her maid. She wanted out of this dress, and she wanted out of it now.

Moments after she called, a tiny woman with greying hair and dancing brown eyes entered the room, curtsying to the princess before coming to her side.

"What do you need, dearie?" the woman asked, her voice croaky and quiet. Jade loved the woman. She had long since dropped all formalities with the princess, aside from the required curtsy.

"Oh, Matilda. Father sent this dress up here to be fitted for when Marquess Jacob arrives. It fits fine, but now I wish to take it off until the ceremony this evening. Would you help me?" Jade asked, mentally chastising the women who had helped her into the dress before promptly disappearing. Likely on her father's orders.

"Oh course, dear. Turn around."

Jade did as she was told and sighed in relief as the last of the corsets strings were pulled away and she could breathe again. Deciding Matilda was as good a person as any to talk to about her problems, she turned around once more.

"Matilda, may I ask you something?" The old woman nodded as she pulled the dress from Jade's shoulders and slid it down to her waist. "What would you do if someone made you wife to a person you could not spend your life with?" The princess turned again as the old woman motioned her to, and she feared she would not answer her.

"Dear, your life is much more complicated than my own. I am free to marry whomever I want, but who would marry an old hag like myself? You are beautiful, child, and smart. Any man would be lucky to have you, and your father knows that, I assure you. He only wants what's best for you."

Jade sighed. A typical answer from a woman working in the palace.

Hearing her sigh, Matilda frowned. "Marquess Jacob is a fine young man, though he may be rough around the edges."

"Marguess Jacob is a whiny toad who only wants me because he thinks I am beautiful. I want a man who sees who I am underneath all the dresses and rouge. The Marquess of Northsbury will not love me. He will wear me on his arm like a prize stag he just killed," Jade replied, stepping out of the dress that now pooled around her feet. She bent to pick it up as Matilda grabbed a wooden hanger for the garment.

"Yes, child, that is all we ever want, is it not? You should feel very lucky. Your father has taken the difficulty of finding a husband off your hands. But, if you really want love, you will not find it in this lifestyle. If you were a peasant girl, love would always rule out over duty." Jade faced the old woman again, her eyes widening. She hadn't expected Matilda to give her such information. The old woman winked at her before leaving, taking the dress with her.

Jade stood motionless for a moment as Matilda's words sunk in. The woman had given her an out. It took the princess only a moment to make her decision. When choosing between becoming Mrs. Marquess Jacob or being free to chose her own life, the decision was simple. An entire world was waiting for her beyond the castle gates; she intended to make it her own.

Ten minutes later, Jade was ready to go. She'd taken a leather bag from her wardrobe and rushed to her brother's room, grabbing various garments from his closet. He'd been away for a few days now and she doubted he'd be back anytime soon. The life he'd chosen upset her, but the decisions he'd made had led to her being free for the first time in her life, so she let it pass for the time being.

As she made her way back to her room, she watched her father's servants scurry around the palace. These people weren't truly free either. Working in the castle, no one had time to start a family. That's why Matilda was nearing her seventies and still never married. She'd been working as the princess's right hand lady since Jade was a child. Matilda had been her first nanny and Jade had clung to the woman like a security blanket ever since.

Hidden away in her room again, she tried to think of a way to sneak her bag past her father. She looked out her window, gauging the drop to the ground. Shrugging, she decided the bag and its contents would survive the fall and hoisted it over the ledge, watching it fall into the hedges below. She looked around her room one last time, making sure she had everything she needed, before looking down at herself.

Jade laughed aloud as she realized she hadn't gotten dressed after Matilda had helped her out of her dress. She was dressed in nothing but undergarments. The princess went to her wardrobe and pulled out a simple yellow dress, slipping it over her head and reveling in the fact no corset was needed.

She tried to look composed as she made her way through the palace, forcing herself not to bolt from the castle. She entered the throne room cautiously, smiling when she saw that her mother had chosen to accompany her father that day. Normally the queen spent her days in the library or the gardens.

"Hello, Mother, Father." Jade curtsied as she reached the silver thrones, smiling at her mother. She then turned her eyes to her father. "I was going to take Bella for a ride. Is that alright?" King Aric never had a problem with Jade riding her black mare, but she made a point to always let her father know where she was. There were dangerous people out there, and it made her feel safer if her father knew where she was.

"Of course, child. Be back by supper, though. We wouldn't want you to miss your big celebration." Aric's grin spread across his weathered face. It had been a rough couple of days, with Duke Aeron being brutally murdered in the palace and his son, Jacob being rushed to Adion. It showed on the king's face that he hadn't been sleeping. It was barely concealed beneath his excitement.

"Yes, Father. Good day, Mother." Jade curtsied once more and forced herself to stroll out of the throne room at a normal pace. Once outside, she didn't hold back, racing across the grounds, laughing as her skirt flowed around her. She was finally free, for the first time in her life. She could go where she wanted, *do* what she wanted. She could go for days without bathing or brushing her hair, let her clothes get dirty and not immediately change.

As Jade neared the stables she slowed, switching back to her princess persona as she ordered Sebastian, their old stable hand, to saddle her beautiful little jennet for her. She found her foot tapping impatiently as she waited for the man, who seemed to be taking his time with Bella that afternoon. As soon as the horse was ready, Jade hurriedly mounted, forcing herself to ride sidesaddle until they left the gates.

She directed Bella to the castle, sneaking her way around to the back. She leapt down, grabbing her bag before climbing back onto the horse. Using a rope she'd taken from the stable, Jade secured the leather bag to Bella's saddle, giving it a tug to make sure it would stay in place. She used the extra large skirt she wore to cover the bag and smiled. She always had been a sneaky little princess.

"Come on, Bella. Let's go and find an adventure!" Jade urged the horse into a steady gallop as soon as the castle gates were behind her, and soon even the town itself began to disappear. She felt a little bit guilty, leaving her father to deal with Jacob on his own, but the man deserved it. A woman deserved to pick her own husband; a woman deserved love.

Jade had every intention of finding it, somewhere out in the world.

"Listen to the musn'ts child. Listen to the don'ts. Listen to the shoudln'ts, the impossible, the won'ts. Listen to the never haves, then listen close to me.... Anything can happen, child. Anything can be."

- Shel Silverstein -

Eight

Richie had been thoroughly scolded for leaving Madam Louise's side in the market place. She swatted the boy on the behind several times on the way back to the palace, but Richie knew she had just been worried. He couldn't blame her for her actions.

As they reached the palace gates, he stole a glance at the worn path through the trees, wishing he could disappear in the forest and stay with Aston. They would have grand adventures together, racing through villages, saving damsels, and reading every book they found along the way. But he had a job to do now.

Madam Louise sent him to his room as soon as they entered the palace. Richie decided to take the long way to his chambers, passing by the throne room on the way. King Donn was there, speaking with someone from the city whom Richie didn't know, though he could not make out what they were saying. With a sigh, he continued to his room, wishing he could do more to help Aston.

"This stinks," he muttered, kicking the door to his room closed. He winced as the sound echoed through the corridor; when no one came to scold him, Richie relaxed again. He made his way to his bed, plopping down on its soft surface and resting his elbows on his knees. He leaned forwards, placing his face in his palms, and swung his legs back and forth.

I have to find a way to help Aston, he thought. It would do him no good sitting around in his room. As much as he disliked the idea of disobeying Madam Louise twice in one day, he knew he had to leave to investigate. Richie stood again, tiptoeing to his door. He would have to be sneaky and sly, like Aston when he went on his missions. The boy grinned, making a game out of the job and turning it into an adventure.

Richie crept down the hallway on his toes, listening for guards and bandits as he made his way through the castle, he thought, narrating his adventure. *If the guards saw him he would be locked in the dungeon, but he had to save the damsel from the ferocious beast.* He was halfway down the hallway now, his face grim.

As he heard approaching footsteps, he crushed himself to the wall, sucking in his stomach and being as still as possible. As soon as the sound was gone, he resumed his mission.

He was almost caught by a dungeon troll, but managed to escape! He slowed his steps as he neared the throne room, listening for the King's even breathing to suggest he was asleep. Due to living in the palace his entire life, Richie knew King Donn took a nap every afternoon, while the sun was at its highest position in the sky. The boy snuck into the room, leaving the doors open just a crack so as not to arouse suspicion.

True to his schedule, King Donn was asleep on his chair. Richie wasn't sure why the king wouldn't return to his room to nap, but he pushed the thought aside as he crept soundlessly down the carpet, stopping in front of the throne.

"If I were a clue, where would I hide?" he asked himself, keeping his voice low. The king was holding an envelope in his hand, but Richie didn't dare try and take it. The rest of the room was clean. He searched around and under all three thrones, looked at all of the columns, and even checked under the rug. Nothing useful was hidden there.

The boy jumped as the door he'd left partially open started to swing inwards. He leapt behind Prince Talbot's throne and made himself as small as possible, his heart racing at the prospect of being caught.

King Donn shifted in his throne, his head falling forwards toward his chest. He jerked awake, shaking his head to clear the last of the drowsiness from his mind. Looking up, he noticed Talbot walking toward him. The king cleared his throat before speaking.

"Talbot, son. What news do you bring?"

Talbot bowed his head at his father before taking a seat in his own throne. "No word, Father. Aston is nowhere to be found. The guard has their best hounds after him now, but we fear he may have crossed the river. If that is true, we won't find his trail." The prince's voice was thick with anger.

Richie cowered behind the throne, silently praying that he wouldn't be caught.

"I am sure they will find him, Talbot. A traitor like that is bound to make a mistake. He's probably still running, leaving this place as far behind as he possibly can. The coward."

"Yes, Father. I am sure you are right. Any word from King Aric? Does he know where the Rogue will strike next?"

Behind the throne, Richie raised his head, his interest peaked. This was the lead he had been waiting for!

"Nothing from King Aric. However, Duke Roland of Northsbury sends word that his king has been targeted. They wish for assistance."

"Do you plan on offering them help, Father?" the prince asked, his tone hopeful.

"I wasn't going to. What do I care of a country so far from our own?" King Donn answered, dismissing the idea with a wave of his hand, which Richie could just see around the side of Talbot's throne.

"Let me go, Father." Silence. Then, Talbot elaborated. "If you were a knight who let a deranged murderer get away and then ran away to avoid your sentence, what would you do?" Another moment of silence followed, and the prince sighed. "Aston will be going after the Rogue, Father. He'll think that bringing the Rogue here will help clear his name of all wrongdoings."

This time, the king answered quickly. "You're absolutely right, Talbot! Go, son. Take as many men with you as you think you might need. Bring Aston back here, alive. I want to speak with him."

Talbot didn't answer, and soon Richie heard the sound of his quickly retreating footsteps. He waited until King Donn fell asleep again, his gentle snores filling the room, before he emerged from his hiding place. Donn had set the envelope on a small table beside his throne and the boy snatched it, tucking it into the waistband of his breeches and pulling his shirt down to conceal it.

As he made his way back to his room, his smile grew larger and larger. Not only could he tell Aston where the Rogue would be

60

next, but he could warn him about Talbot's army too. It was more than he could ask for! Richie would be the greatest spy Aston had ever seen. In five days time he would be with the knight again, telling him all the wonderful news. His mentor would find the Rogue, bring him back, and live happily as a knight again!

Richie bumped into Madam Louise as his thoughts got away from him. He oomphed, falling on his behind on the stone floors. Madam Louise placed her hands on her hips and sent him a stern look.

"What are you doing out of your room, young man?" she scolded. The boy smiled up at her and shrugged, ever the picture of innocence. With a sigh, Madam Louise helped him to his feet. "While you're here, you may as well help me. Come along. We are going to the gardens to find vegetables for tonight's stew."

Richie tagged along happily, for once not bothered by his work. He picked the largest, ripest vegetables he could find before heading back inside, helping Madam Louise clean countless rooms before falling into bed that night. As he slept, he dreamt of Aston on wild adventures with a beautiful maiden by his side. He knew, somehow, that what he saw was real, and that Aston would he truly free someday soon.

"There is a woman at the beginning of all great things."
- Alphonse de Lamartine –

Nine

Jade ran Bella as hard and fast as she could through the mild, fall night. The horse's frantic breathing did nothing to calm her own pounding heart. Two days had passed since she'd left home, and she regretted the decision more with each passing moment. Night had fallen; the forest's creatures came alive as moonlight filtered through the treetops. Risking a glance behind her, Jade barely held in her scream.

Racing after her black mare was a pack of wolves, the alpha so close Jade could see the yellow of his eyes. He nipped at Bella's hind leg and the horse let out a squeal, running faster, pounding her hooves into the hard ground. Jade gripped the reins tighter, wishing she were home in bed instead of in the middle of the forest, running for her life. Bella stumbled and Jade barely caught herself, leaning low over her steed's back and ushering the horse forward with whispered words.

What am I doing? I don't belong here! Jade thought, her eyes wide as she looked back again. The wolves were falling behind, some branching off to the sides. They were going to try and surround her. A fierce howl ripped through the night, mixing with the sound of Bella's frantic panting and the thundering of her hooves against the packed ground. Jade looked around herself, hoping to see something familiar, but it was a wasted effort.

She had no idea where she was. As a lady who'd lived her entire life inside castle walls, the forest was completely foreign to her. Everything looked the same; green trees, their trunks grey in the twilight, worn out paths leading in every direction. She wouldn't be able to find her way home, even if she wanted to return. Jade wished something would appear to her, some sign telling her where to go. She turned around to look for the wolves that had been chasing her and was surprised at what she found.

The majority of the wolf pack had disappeared. Only one was left, quickly catching up to her as Bella started to tire. Jade took a deep breath before screaming as loud as she could. "Somebody help!" She received no reply, but she hadn't expected to. As Bella slowed, Jade crashed into a clearing, an almost perfect circle of the forest where all of the trees had been roughly chopped away. She caught sight of a man standing up as the wolf trailing her jumped into the clearing behind her.

She entered the forest again on the opposite side of the clearing and started to slow Bella as she realized the wolf was no longer following her. Jade turned Bella around and went back toward the clearing, forcing her horse into a trot. She stopped at the edge of the trees, staying hidden in the shadows.

The man she had seen was standing about fifteen feet away from the wolf. A silver blade shone in the moonlight in his left hand as he circled the grey creature. The wolf had his mouth slightly open, his teeth bared as he contemplated attacking the man. His decision made, the wolf pounced. Jade screamed but realized her fear was misplaced. The wolf ran straight onto the man's blade, red staining the ground. It was over as quickly as it had started. The man knelt down, wiping his blade clean on the grass, and then stood, staring off into the forest.

After another moment of gazing into the trees, his head lowered and he turned in her direction. Jade hopped down from Bella and cocked her head to the side, studying the man. The trees thinned over the clearing, leaving an almost perfect circle for the moonlight to filter through. The man before her was tall, muscular, and weary looking. He had a week's growth of beard on his face and his hair was a tangled mess. His eyes had flashed cobalt blue in the moonlight, but Jade assumed they were lighter in the daytime.

A howl ripped through the quiet of the night and Jade shivered, wondering if the wolves were still after her. She looked at Bella, noticing the way the mare's eyes widened in fear at the sound. Jade needed someone to look after her,to protect her. Maybe the man before her was the sign she had been waiting for.

With a sigh and a quick straightening of her dress, Jade strode into the clearing.

**

Aston stared at the woman he'd saved as she walked toward him. She was a petite woman, her head stopping just under his chin. She wore a yellow dress that was torn at the hem, probably from riding through the forest. Her hair was partly up and partly down, tangled with sticks and leaves. Aston would have laughed at her appearance were he sure he didn't look just as haggard. He stood staring at her, waiting for something to happen, for her to speak or to leave.

Neither human spoke, though their horses seemed relaxed. Sterling, tied to a tree at the far end of the clearing, perked his ears at the appearance of the mare. Bella, in turn, whinnied a hello to the grey stallion. When Aston was sure the woman wouldn't speak first, he decided to introduce himself.

"My lady, may I ask what you are doing in the forest at this time of night?" he began. Better to find out who she was before revealing his identity. If she'd heard of his misdeeds, she would run screaming from the clearing and most likely bring him nothing but trouble.

"You may ask, but that does not guarantee I will answer," she replied, her tone curt.

"I suppose it doesn't. Very well, be on your way. I won't stop you." Aston sat back down on his stump, wanting nothing more than to be left in peace. Richie would be coming the next day, and he intended to wait on his stump until the boy appeared. Having the woman around would only complicate things.

"I ran away from my life. Satisfied?" the woman answered, walking her horse further into the clearing.

"No. What life?" Aston asked.

The woman rolled her eyes. "If I told you that, I would have to run again." At Aston's curious glance, she added, "You would make me go back and I refuse to go. It is better and easier for both of us if you don't know."

Aston shrugged and looked away.

"Why are you out here, sir?" she asked, and Aston's shoulders tensed.

"The same reason you are I suppose; I ran away from my life." Aston suddenly understood why the woman would not share details with him. If he told her who he was, why he was running, she would turn him in herself.

"Then we are at an understanding. My name is Jade. Thank you for saving me," she offered, taking a seat on the ground and leaning against the stump Aston still occupied.

"Aston. It's a pleasure, my lady, I am sure," he replied. He wanted Jade to leave, firstly because he she asked too many questions, and secondly because he wanted to keep her safe. Annoying as she was, she was still a woman. And he was still a knight.

"Why are you sitting here, Aston?" Jade asked.

"I am waiting on news," he replied. The woman, Jade, was getting more comfortable. She didn't seem to want to leave. This was just what he needed.

"News of what?"

"News of The Rogue Royal." Aston didn't miss the way she sucked in a breath at the name. "Oh yes, he is a very dangerous man. And I am hunting him. Shouldn't you be getting along to wherever you were going?" He didn't want to be rude to a woman, but she was being persistent and nosy, two things his life would best avoid right now.

"I am aware of who he is," Jade announced, and Aston thought he saw her flinch. "Why are you hunting him?"

"He condemned me. Well, Prince…it's a long and tiring story. Nothing you should be bothered with."

"Okay…I suppose I will get some rest while you are being stubborn. Do you have an extra blanket?" Aston almost told Jade no, he did not have a blanket, nor did he enjoy her company. Instead he decided the woman had had a rough enough day and allowed her use of a blanket and his company for the night. He would rid himself of her the next day.

As morning dawned, Jade stretched. Her neck and shoulders ached, her back was stiff, and there were tree bark indentions on her cheek.

"Well, that's the last time *I* sleep on the ground," she announced, standing and pushing her arms as high above her head as she could reach.

"You won't be sticking around for long, then," Aston said, and she whirled around to face him. She'd almost forgotten she had company.

"You do this often?" At Aston's nod, she frowned. "Don't you have a home?"

Aston pointed at himself. "Runaway, remember? I *used* to have a home. Now, I live wherever my journey takes me."

As romantic and enticing as *that* sounded, Jade did *not* want to live in the forest. Unless she had a cabin, a fireplace, a kitchen, and a bed, that is. "Doesn't it get tiring, sleeping outside and eating...grass?" she asked, looking around herself. No fruit trees, no berry bushes. Nothing but oak trees and pine needles.

"Sterling eats grass. I eat meat," Aston replied, producing a rabbit from behind his back. The princess gagged at the bloodied animal and closed her eyes.

"How do you eat that?" she questioned, opening one eye to look back at Aston. He'd set the hare on the ground and was starting to skin it. She quickly closed her eye again and turned around. "Where's Bella?" she added, suddenly noticing her horse was nowhere to be found.

"You went to sleep last night without tying her up. As soon as she heard a wolf howl, she took off," he answered.

"She what?! How could you let her run away?" Jade snapped, turning around again. This time the rabbit didn't bother her; she was too furious to pay attention to what Aston was doing.

"Excuse me, what? How could *I* let her run away? I believe she was *your* horse, *your* responsibility; not mine," he sneered.

"Well, I was sleeping," she retaliated, folding her arms across her chest and sticking her nose in the air.

"Look here, *Princess*. I don't know who you think you are, but I am not your servant," Aston barked, dropping his knife and the rabbit on the ground and standing. He towered over Jade and she swallowed, his mention of the word 'princess' causing her momentary panic.

"What did you call me?" she asked, her voice shaking. Was she really that obvious?

"Princess. It's what you're acting like. Stuck up, arrogant, with no responsibility. If I didn't know any better, I would say you were royalty," he told her, his face full of disdain.

He didn't move away from her and Jade felt suddenly egotistical. Stuck up? Arrogant? She'd never seen herself that way. She had always seen herself as kind and thoughtful. Looking back on the short time she'd spent with Aston, she could understand why he saw differently.

Finally finding strength in herself, Jade tore her gaze from his and looked at the ground. She could feel tears burning her eyes, but she refused to let them fall.

"I'm sorry. I know it wasn't your fault. I was just so tired last night, and there were wolves chasing me. I've never been away from home before and I am used to people doing things for me. I shouldn't have yelled at you like that." One of the tears she was holding back fell from her eye, but Jade wiped it away quickly. "Bella has been my horse for five years. She was the only part of my life I had left."

Aston studied her for a moment. Jade could feel his eyes appraising her. She resisted the urge to squirm. It seemed an eternity passed before he moved. He sighed and walked away from her and over to his horse, grabbing his reins. Then he walked back to Jade and handed the reins to her, looking away as her surprised face looked up to meet his.

"What are you doing?" she asked him.

Aston shook his head. "I don't know. Helping you, I guess. His name is Sterling," he said, motioning to the horse. "He'll take you wherever you need to go. Just, don't go to Fridel. He's too easily recognized there," Aston added, almost as an afterthought.

"I can't take your horse. Besides, I'm not going anywhere," Jade said, pushing the reins back into Aston's hand.

"Aren't going anywhere? You can't stay *here*," Aston said, his voice incredulous.

"Of course I can. I'm a free woman. I can do whatever I like," Jade responded. "I'm lonely and know nothing about hunting or…killing things," she choked out, her eyes turning to the rabbit on the ground, half skinned. With a shiver, she looked back up at Aston. "You could teach me to take care of myself. And maybe I could help you out in return, somehow." At Aston's incredulous look Jade frowned.

"Help me? Do what? Sew?" Aston laughed as Jade scowled. *Sew? The nerve of him!*

"No! Maybe I could help you find The Rogue Royal!" Aston stopped laughing at Jade's words, his eyes narrowing as a dark shadow passed over his face.

"I won't let you anywhere near him. You might be irritating and loud, but you're still a woman and as a kni…as a man of honor I will not let harm come to you." Aston barely caught his tongue, but Jade understood anyway.

"A *knight*? Why is a *knight* hiding in the forest?" she questioned, her voice loud.

"And we are back to the questions I will not answer about myself," he answered, kneeling on the ground and returning to his rabbit.

Jade scoffed and sat on the stump, crossing her legs at the knee. Aston sent her a questioning gaze and she shrugged; she didn't feel like being ladylike.

"Aston! Aston!" She looked up at the young voice echoing through the trees. Aston winced. A young boy raced into the clearing on the back of a tall white stallion, jumping down and running to Aston. He jumped on the knight's back and almost caused the knight to fall onto his kill.

"Calm down, Richie, and don't scream so loud. You'll get me killed," Aston laughed, rubbing the boy's head.

"Guess what, guess what!? I know where the Rogue is going next!" Richie exclaimed, jumping up and down. Jade and Aston both perked up at his words.

"Where?" Aston asked.

Richie grinned. "Nothsbury! Duke Roland sent word! The Rogue plans on killing the king! Oh, and Talbot is bringing an army to try and find you, so be careful!" Richie said.

Aston looked sideways at Jade , like gauge her reaction to the news, but she pretended to be occupied with the hem of her dress. "Thank you, Richie. You've done great. Don't come back here until I send you a message, okay? I don't want anyone getting suspicious and following you here."

"Okay, Aston. Oh! I almost forgot! I took this letter from King Donn too. He hasn't opened it yet and he will probably know it's gone. It just arrived today, but I thought it might be important," Richie said, reaching into his pants pocket and withdrawing the creased envelope. Aston nodded, looking at the scrawled writing across the back of the cream colored parchment. Stretching her neck, Jade saw it was a letter from her father.

"Who's she?" Richie asked, leaning close and whispering in Aston's ear. Jade barely heard him.

"Her name is Jade. That's all I know about her," Aston answered, standing and going to Sterling. He watched out of the corner of his eye as the boy sauntered over to Jade.

Jade looked down at the boy approaching her. His face was red and freckled, his red hair filthy and matted. He was the most adorable child she had ever seen, strutting over to her with his chest puffed out. He held out a dirty hand to her, which she took in her own, laughing as he leaned down to press sticky lips to the back of her hand. She cringed internally, but quickly shook off the reaction. If she was going to travel with Aston, she would have to get used to dirt.

"Hello, Lady Jade. I am Sir Richard," he said, forcing his voice to sound older, deeper.

Jade laughed on the inside, but tried to remain stoic on the outside. "Well, hello, Sir Richard. It is an honor to meet you," she said, standing to curtsy to the boy, who bowed low in return.

With the formalities gone, Richie's face grew into a wide grin, revealing three gaps where teeth were missing. "You are very pretty, Lady Jade," he said.

"Well, thank you. You are quite handsome," she replied, grabbing the boy around the middle and pulling him into her lap.

"Are you going to help Aston be free again?" Richie asked.

Jade looked up at the knight, noticing the way he quickly turned his head from them; he'd been eavesdropping. "I hope so, Richard. What happened?" she asked, trusting the child to tell her. She saw Aston flinch but ignored it; she had this powerful urge to help the man, a force within her telling her it was what she was meant to do.

"A bad man got away from him. Prince Talbot blamed everything on Aston, even though it was all Talbot's fault. He's a dirty prince," Richie explained.

"I see. Well, thank you for telling me, Richard."

"Are you a princess?" Richie whispered, and Jade stilled.

"Why do you say that?" Jade asked the boy. Was she really so obvious? Aston had seemed to believe she wasn't. Children always were more perceptive than adults though. They saw the world so differently.

"You're really pretty, your dress is better made than the ones Madam Louise makes, and your eyes are lined with kohl. Madam Louise says only really wealthy women can afford to be all made up," Richie explained. He leaned in closer to Jade to whisper in her ear. "Plus, I've had dreams lately, dreams where Aston meets a beautiful princess and they go on adventures together."

When Richie pulled away, his eyes wide in expectancy of her answer, Jade thought for a moment. She knew about Aston, about why he was searching for the Rogue. Would it hurt for the boy to know she was a princess? In answer to Richie's question, she nodded. His smile returned and he hugged her, wrapping his grimy arms around her neck and squeezing gently.

"Help him be free," he whispered, before scampering off to Aston's side. "I brought you Edward 'cause I thought you might need him," he told Aston. Aston nodded and ruffled the boy's hair. After a quick goodbye and a heartfelt hug, Richie left Jade and Aston in silence.

Jade watched Aston fiddling with the horses, tugging on their reins and checking their saddles. She could tell he wanted to ask her something.

Finally, he turned. "So...I guess you don't have any questions I can't answer now."

"You're a runaway knight."

A quick nod from Aston confirmed. "You're really intent on coming with me?" he asked. When Jade nodded, he pointed her to the white stallion. "Up you go, then. We have a quick stop to make along the way." At Jade's questioning look, he said, "We need to get you some clothes. And a bath."

Jade scoffed and turned away from Aston. He smiled and climbed on Sterling's back, tucking the envelope from Richie into his satchel to read later.

"There is nothing like returning to a place that remains unchanged to find the ways in which you yourself have altered".
— Nelson Mandela —

Ten

The trees were thickly packed together in this part of the forest, barely allowing room for their horses to walk through. Over head, birds sang in the highest branches of pine and cypress, saluting the morning. Quiet, melodic tinkling could be heard from the water running through a nearby brook. The sun shone lightly through the canopy of tree limbs, making small, well-lit patches between the dark shadows of low-hanging branches. Across the path, various flowers wound and flowed. Pink, red, yellow, and white decorated the thick grass decorating the forest floor. A light wind pulled at Jade's hair, gently whipping it into her face before pushing it back again.

She tried not to stare at Aston's back on their ride to…wherever he was taking her. He hadn't said much to her since their exchange that morning, and she feared he was still angry. She hadn't meant to act so spoiled; as a princess, it was almost second nature. Deciding it had been quiet long enough, Jade urged her stallion forward so that she was riding next to Aston instead of behind him.

Aston spared a glance in her direction before putting his eyes forward again. "Yes?"

"Oh..um.." Jade hadn't expected him to say something first. She was still trying to think of a topic for conversation. "I was just…wondering…um… why did you run away?"

"I thought Richie explained everything to you," Aston said, glancing at her again.

Jade blushed and looked down. "He did, sort of. I just wanted to hear it from you, I guess."

Aston sighed, but relented. Jade wished she could see into his mind and figure out what he was thinking. "I worked for King Donn in Fridel. I've been a knight for three years. Well, I guess I *had* been a knight. I don't think I can use the title anymore." At this, a frown graced Aston's features, but he shook it off and continued. "I've never failed a mission and some of the other men hated me for it. They said I was too kind-hearted. It never bothered me. I didn't realize how much Prince Talbot hated me, though."

"Why do you think the prince hated you?" Jade asked, her curiosity peaking. She wanted to know everything about the man beside her.

"He's the one who lied to King Donn and told him *I* was the one who failed in my duties." When she continued to stare at him, Aston sighed. "Talbot and I were sent to Adion to stop The Rogue Royal from murdering Duke Aeron." Jade stiffened; Aston didn't seem to notice. "A woman screamed while we were sneaking into the palace and Talbot took off, hoping to save a damsel, I suppose. I followed him, saw the Rogue leave the room across the hall, and chased him until I lost him. Talbot, of course, wouldn't take the blame and placed his actions upon my shoulders. Which led to me being sentenced to hang. Well, that and the fact that I was…less than cordial to the king when reprimanded me. So, I ran."

Jade didn't speak when he was finished with his story. She didn't have the heart to tell him what she was thinking. Instead, she switched topics.

"Richie seems to really like you. Is he your brother?"

Aston laughed aloud at Jade's question. "No, no. He's not family. Not by blood, anyway. He needed someone to look up to, someone to take care of him. I just happened to be the first one who was willing to do so. Can I ask you something?"

Jade nodded but didn't look up.

"Who are you?"

"I already told you. My name is Jade," she answered, staring straight ahead to avoid Aston's searching eyes.

"Don't give me that. You know that's not what I was asking."

Jade shook her head, refusing to answer. When she looked up again, Aston was pulling Sterling to a stop. They were in a clearing, but they weren't alone. A small cabin sat in front of them and, as soon as they arrived, a plump little woman came rushing out of the house. Aston climbed down from Sterling and the woman ran into his arms, sobbing.

"Aston Smith, I should beat you for scaring us like that! What were you thinking!?" she cried. Aston smiled, rubbing the woman's back, while Jade looked on in confusion.

A tall, burly man stepped from the cabin next, walking towards Aston with a frown on his face. "I told you to wait," he said.

Aston only shook his head. "I'm sorry, Delgrab. You know why I couldn't stay."

Delgrab nodded. "Why are you back?" Aston turned his head to the side and Delgrab looked at Jade for the first time. "Who's she?"

"Her name is Jade. That's all I know," Aston said.

Jade blushed; it sounded so awful when he said it like that, but it was the truth. That *was* all he knew about her. She dismounted and strode toward the man, determined not to look as nervous as she felt. She held a hand out to Delgrab, who grasped it and kissed it while she curtsied. "It's a pleasure," she said.

Delgrab nodded. "The pleasure is mine, I'm sure."

A sharp *smack* resounded from beside them, and Jade jumped, turning to look at Aston. The plump little woman was holding her left hand with her right, storming away towards the cabin. Aston's head was turned to the side, his cheek red, but he was smiling.

Delgrab winced. "She was really mad," he offered.

Aston nodded, laughed, and went after the woman.

Jade looked back at Delgrab. "What was that about?" she asked him.

The man turned to her and grimaced before offering Jade his arm, which she accepted, and directing her toward the house. He grabbed Sterling's reins and those of the white stallion in his other hand. "You should go inside and make sure Alys doesn't kill him." Jade's eyes widened, and Delgrab laughed. "She wouldn't *really* kill him…I think. But, to be on the safe side…"

Delgrab withdrew his arm from Jade's and headed around the cabin. Jade stayed where she was for a moment looking in the direction the man had disappeared in before following Aston inside.

Aston sat at a small wooden table with the woman named Alys across from him. They were speaking in low voices when Jade approached. Aston looked up at her and, for the first time, she really noticed him.

Alys had obviously allowed him use of Delgrab's razor. His clean-shaven skin was tanned and perfect, no trace of scars or battle wounds. His eyes were dark blue, just a shade lighter than they had been when she'd seen him in the forest the night before. His shaggy hair was dust colored, not quite blonde, but not quite brown. He smiled at her, revealing rows of perfect white teeth and she felt her heart flutter in her chest. It was only when he said her name questioningly that she realized he had been talking to her.

"I'm sorry…what?" she asked, feeling ignorant.

"I said, Alys is going to take some measurements from you so she can make you a dress. Is that alright?" Aston asked again.

Jade shook her head. "No more dresses." At Aston's puzzled glance, she elaborated. "They get in the way in the woods. If I'm right, I have a feeling I will be spending a lot of time riding. Breeches and a tunic would be nice, though," she finished. Alys grunted but agreed, grabbing Jade by the arm and dragging her into a back room for privacy.

**

Shortly after the door closed behind Alys and Jade, Delgrab came inside. He sat at the table across from Aston, folding his arms on the tabletop.

"Who is she?" he asked again.

Aston shook his head. "I honestly have no idea, Delgrab. I went back to Fridel to talk to Richie and she just appeared in the middle of the forest, in the middle of the night, no less. She plopped herself down beside me and went to sleep. She hasn't left me alone since."

Delgrab laughed and shook his head. "She sounds like a handful. What are you going to do with her?"

The knight shrugged, looking back at the room where the two women had disappeared. "I don't know, Delgrab. I can't just *abandon* her. She'd never make it on her own. Plus, she knows too much about me and now she knows this place. If she turns on me and leaves, you and I will both be in trouble."

Delgrab nodded in agreement. Alys and Jade took that moment to reenter. Aston turned to look at Jade and found himself staring.

He'd never seen a woman in men's clothing before; seeing Jade, he wondered why more women didn't wear them. She was slim in the waist and curvy everywhere else; the pants and blouse showed off her slim figured more than any dress ever could. The white shirt was tucked into the pants, tightening the top over her chest and stomach. Her brown breeches fit snug on her hips and flowed loosely around her legs before tightening right above her ankles, showing off the black riding boots she'd been wearing under her dress.

"Will this work okay?" Jade asked. Unable to speak, Aston nodded.

"Are those mine?" Delgrab grumbled. Alys and Jade glanced at each other before laughing. Aston joined in; Delgrab was the only one who found nothing funny about a woman wearing his clothes.

"Oh, sweetheart, you're just mad because she looks better in them than you do," Alys teased, patting her husband on the cheek before heading into the kitchen. Jade followed, unsure of what else to do.

"Alys?" she asked once the two women were alone. Alys looked up at her, her approval for Jade to continue. "Has Aston always been so....serious?"

Alys looked somber for a moment before going back to her cooking, answering without looking at Jade. "He used to be more fun, more free. King Donn has made him live a rough life, and that no good son of his hasn't helped either."

"What do you mean?"

"Some of the women in town used to talk, dear, passing around information they'd heard from their husbands. They'd say King Donn sent Aston on missions *hoping* he would fail. Talbot never liked Aston, so Donn always hoped he would mess up and condemn himself. This last offense was just what he'd been waiting for. I don't understand politics, dear. Aston is the most kind and helpful person I know, aside from my Del. I don't know why anyone would ever want to hurt him."

"I know what you mean," Jade said, her mind somewhere else. She wondered if her father knew about King Donn's methods. Why make a man a knight, only to want him to fail?

"Speaking of hurting him, I won't allow it," Alys said. Jade looked up at the woman, stunned. "I love that man as much as I love Delgrab, and I won't stand to see anyone hurting him. I let

King Donn do it because there was nothing I could do to stop it. Keep that in mind."

Jade could tell by the look on Alys' face that she was completely serious. The knife she had been chopping vegetables with suddenly looked a lot more dangerous. Swallowing thickly, Jade nodded. Alys smiled at her and went back to cooking; Jade wondered just what she'd gotten herself into.

**

Alys and Delgrab insisted Jade and Aston spend the night. It surprised Jade when Aston agreed; she'd suspected he would want to leave as soon as possible, before King Donn's soldiers came knocking on Delgrab's door. Aston, however, didn't seem worried.

After a fulfilling dinner, the four adjourned to the cabin's living area, Delgrab and Alys on the handcrafted couch, Aston and Jade in chairs on the opposite side of the room. Delgrab had lit a fire and Alys had given Jade a blanket to ward off the night's chill.

"Where will you two go now?" Delgrab asked. Jade turned to Aston for an answer.

"We have reason to believe that the Rogue will be going after the king of Northsbury. That's where we will go." Delgrab nodded.

Alys frowned. "You're going after that dangerous murderer? Are you out of your mind, Aston? Bringing a lady on such a mission…"

"It's fine, Lady Alys," Jade said, rushing to make sure the woman wouldn't hit Aston again. "He told me before what he planned to do, and I agreed to help him. I made a promise to," she said, looking at Aston. He smiled at her, but it didn't reach his eyes. He was thinking about his past again, she presumed. His eyes were dark with worry, and his fists were clenched on the arm of the chair he occupied.

"Hmph. I don't understand you, Jade. You are beautiful and obviously high class. What were you doing in the forest in the middle of the night?" At Alys's pointed question, Aston looked curiously at Jade.

She squirmed in her chair before answering. "I took Bella out for a ride, but...we got lost," she lied. She needed to think of a proper lie to tell Aston, but she hoped this would work for now.

"You got lost? Child, how often do you ride in the woods?"

"Never?" Jade's answer sounded more like a question, but she tried not to show her disappointment on her face. She knew everyone could see right through her, but she hoped they wouldn't push.

Aston saved her. "We should get some rest," he said, standing. Delgrab did the same, as did Jade.

Alys looked unsatisfied, but stood as well. "Will you two be sharing a bed, then?" she asked.

Jade could feel her cheeks heating up at the woman's words. She sneaked a look at Aston, almost happy to see that the idea surprised him as much as it had her. His jaw had dropped, and his eyes were wider than normal. The blush that marred her cheeks wasn't evident on Aston, but he was making a weird flapping motion with his mouth, almost like a fish. He was sputtering, trying to answer, but words evaded him.

Delgrab laughed. "That'll be a no, Alys," he answered, saving Aston the trouble of forming a coherent thought.

"I'll take the couch," Aston said, finally finding his voice. Though it was higher pitched than usual. Delgrab and Alys stepped away from the piece of furniture and allowed the knight room to lay down. He threw a hand across his slightly reddened face as soon as his back hit the hand-sewn cushions.

"I'll show you to your room, dear," Alys said, taking Jade by her elbow and leading her out of the room.

Delgrab walked to Aston's side and slapped his friend on the shoulder, successfully removing Aston's arm from his face. "Sorry about her…you know how she is."

Aston sent a glare to his friend before sighing, smiling up at his friend. He knew Alys too well to hold a grudge. The woman just wanted him to be happy. The knight smiled as he watched Delgrab leave the room. He'd thought to never see his two friends again, yet here he was, six days later. His life hadn't changed as much as he thought it had. He still had what mattered most in the world.

Friends.

> *"Tis not seasonable to call a man a traitor that has an army at his heels."*
> - John Selden -

Eleven

Ernst strode through Northsbury, fingering the dagger at his waist. He had one more night before his next kill called. One more night that the King of Northsbury could lie in his bed and know he was safe. He glanced around the street, taking in the cracked cobblestones, the houses that were falling apart, the starving citizens. King Roland deserved what was coming to him. No king should let his people go to waste like this. No king was above his charges.

"Ernst!"

At the sound of his name, Ernst turned and found himself gazing up into Prince Talbot's face. "Talbot, old friend," he said, walking forward to grasp Talbot's hand as he jumped down from Red, and the two fell into step beside each other.

"Ernst! It's been a while! What are you doing in Summerslade, so far away from home?" Talbot asked, holding Red's reins and walking with Ernst. Ernst shrugged.

"Business. Pleasure. Isn't it all the same?" he answered, his mouth turning up into a crooked smile.

Talbot grinned. "It has been," he replied.

"What about you, Talbot? What brings you here so late in the year? You and Donn don't normally appear around these parts until the holiday ball."

"Oh, well, I'm here on official business. Father sent me," Talbot replied, puffing his chest out.

"Oh? What's so important that Donn would send his son?" Ernst asked, his brow furrowing.

Talbot leaned in close before answering. "The Rogue Royal and a runaway knight."

Ernst raised an eyebrow. "Elaborate?"

Talbot grinned and leaned back again. "The Rogue Royal murdered Duke Aeron in Adion. Aston Smith of Fridel let the man get away by turning his attention to a woman instead of the murderer. Aston was found guilty of treason and sentenced to be hanged, but he ran. I've been sent to retrieve him."

"And you think he will be here, in Northsbury?" Ernst asked, his voice incredulous. He remembered the knight chasing after him. He hadn't seemed the traitorous type.

Talbot nodded. "We have reason to believe he will chase down the Rogue and try to capture him to clear his name."

Ernst flinched. "That doesn't sound like Aston. He's always been the careful knight. Why throw everything away for a woman?"

Talbot laughed aloud. "Aston didn't do anything wrong. *I'm* the one who let the murderer get away."

"But you said--"

"I know what I said, Ernst. I *lied*. I couldn't tell my father I'm the reason his closest friend is now dead. Or that I did it all to save a princess. So I lied. Aston was the only person there who

86

could take the blame, so he did." Talbot said, standing tall as if proud of himself for his cleverness.

"Wow, Talbot. Sounds like you really thought that out," Ernst said, trying to keep his voice even. He'd been a close "friend" of Talbot's for years, and he had always known the prince was lazy and irresponsible. He hadn't, however, known Talbot was capable of condemning a man to save himself. Thinking about it now, Ernst realized it was completely in Talbot's character to do so.

"I did. I spent the ride home from Adion trying to think of something to tell my father. I realize he wouldn't have killed me, but I still didn't want to deal with him over something so…trivial."

"Duke Aeron's death was trivial to you?" Ernst asked, his voice incredulous. While he had been the one to kill the duke, it was everyone else's duty to mourn. He looked down at the black ribbon tied around his upper arm and sighed. He hated having to publicly mourn the people he killed, but it couldn't be helped. He couldn't have anyone asking questions.

"It was Duke Aeron, Ernst. He was stuck up and perverted. Everyone knew that. Lady Viola knew that, but she still stayed with him. Isn't that why he was targeted? Does the Rogue kill people who don't deserve to die?"

Ernst frowned. Yes, in his mind, the Duke had deserved his fate. Talbot was the only person who seemed to agree with him.

"I suppose he doesn't. Do you fear for your life, Talbot?"

The prince looked at Ernst questionably. "Why should I?"

"Well, you seem to fit the profile. Arrogant, selfish, and uncaring; you'd make the perfect target for the Rogue."

Talbot scoffed. "I don't think so, Ernst. I have no say in the world. The Rogue only kills people with the power to make bad things happen."

"What about Prince Orion? He was in the same position as you, but the Rogue still killed him."

Talbot shrugged. "Prince Orion's father was on the verge of death. He would have ascended the throne soon."

"You have an answer for everything, don't you, Talbot?" Ernst asked, smiling his crooked grin.

"Always. Now, what say you we head to the palace? If Aston wants to catch the Rogue, the palace is the perfect place to start."

Ernst nodded and followed after Talbot. He pulled his cloak closer to his body, fingering the dagger at his waist. If it wouldn't have blown his cover and ruined his plans, he would have killed Talbot then and there. Instead, he would do what he had come to do. He would kill the king, and then he'd make plans to go to Fridel, where his next target would be waiting for him.

Talbot wouldn't have to worry about his life or his problem with Aston Smith for much longer.

"You never really leave a place or person you love; part of them you take with you, leaving a part of yourself behind."
- Unknown Author -

Twelve

Aston woke the next morning to laughter coming from the kitchen. He stretched and yawned, blinking the last of his dream from his eyes. He sat up slowly and looked around, momentarily forgetting where he was. Delgrab walked by and clapped him on the shoulder.

"Morning," he said, continuing towards the kitchen.

"Morning," Aston yawned in response. He stood and followed Delgrab, wondering what the commotion in the kitchen was about. He stifled a laugh when he walked into the chaos.

Alys and Jade were standing in the middle of the room, covered in flour. As Aston watched, Alys grabbed a handful and threw it at Jade, laughing as Jade squealed and ducked around the corner, running into Aston. Aston caught her by the shoulders and held her away from him, not wanting to clean her mess with his shirt.

"Morning," he laughed, raising an eyebrow at her appearance.

Jade looked behind her, smiling when she saw Delgrab holding Alys in the middle of the kitchen. "Morning...excuse me," she said, stepping out of his arms and going toward the wash room.

Alys followed her after planting a soft kiss on the tip of Delgrab's nose.

Aston shook his head as the women walked away and entered the kitchen, offering to help Delgrab clean while Alys and Jade washed up.

"What was that about?" Aston asked.

Delgrab shrugged. "Who knows? Alys told me she was going to wake Jade and make breakfast. Next thing I knew, I heard laughing, screaming, and squealing. And now I have a mess to clean up." Though Delgrab tried to appear angered, Aston could see the light in his eyes saying he was more amused.

"Jade and I have to leave today. You understand that, right?"

Delgrab nodded. "You have to get to Northsbury before King Roland is killed."

This time, it was Aston's turn to nod. He looked at his friend with a determined fire in his eyes. "The Rogue might be the only person who can clear my name. If he caught any glimpse of me…"

"I understand. Do you really think he'll waltz up to King Donn and say 'I'm The Rogue Royal. Your son is incompetent?'"

Aston laughed aloud. "No, Delgrab. I don't know what I'm thinking. I just know I have to try, and that catching the Rogue is the only thing I can think of right now."

Jade emerged from the washroom then dressed in her white blouse and brown pants and came to say goodbye to Delgrab.

"I'm assuming we are leaving now?" she asked Aston.

"After a quick breakfast, of course," Alys announced as she came back into the room.

The look in her eyes told Aston that he would do best not to argue. He nodded. "Of course, Alys, after breakfast."

The woman smiled and went to her kitchen. Sounds of cooking could be heard soon after: simmering bacon, crackling fire, and the clanking of pans. It didn't take Alys long to have everyone seated at the table and eating their fill. Aston excused himself while Jade was still eating to prepare the horses.

Jade helped Alys with the dishes before turning to Delgrab. "Thank you for everything," she said, smiling at him. She wanted to hug the big bear of a man, but she still felt a little uncomfortable. She knew that Aston trusted these people with his life, but she was still a stranger to them.

"You are welcome here anytime, lass," he said, placing a chaste kiss on the back of her hand. Jade left then, going into the back to say her farewells to Alys as well.

Delgrab walked outside, where Aston was already waiting for Jade, the horses ready to go. The knight grabbed his friend in a hug. "Goodbye for now, Delgrab."

Delgrab leaned in close to Aston, whispering in his ear. "You take care of her, Aston. She needs you."

Aston nodded at his friend, a small smile gracing his features. "I will."

Alys came out of the cabin and grabbed the knight in a hug, squeezing his arms to his sides. Aston laughed, pushing Alys back and giving her a gentle hug in return.

"You be safe, Aston Smith. Do you hear me?" she scolded, tears in her eyes.

Aston nodded. "I will, Alys. I'm going to fix this, I promise." Seemingly convinced, Alys smiled at him, pulling him forward and giving him a light kiss on the cheek. Jade came out of the cabin and walked over to her stallion, clambering on. Aston followed suit, hoisting himself onto Sterling. With one last look at Delgrab and Alys, standing arm in arm in the cabin's front yard, Aston and Jade rode into the forest.

**

"How far is Northsbury from Fridel?" Jade asked Aston.

Aston frowned. "It's almost a two day ride. I'm afraid we can only rest as long as the horses need to. I can't afford to miss the Rogue."

Jade nodded and turned away. The Rogue Royal was a touchy subject for her. She needed to tell Aston what she knew, but she feared he would abandon her. Instead, she kept her secrets inside. "I guess it's good that we stayed with Delgrab and Alys, then. It was nice, sleeping in a real bed, having dinner with real friends."

"That won't happen very often as long as you're with me, Jade. I don't have friends aside from Delgrab and Alys. Even in the palace, I was always alone," Aston warned her.

"I don't mind. I'm sorry I was a bit…stuck up when we met. I've never been on my own before. I've always had my parents around to take care of me," Jade apologized.

Aston met her gaze and smiled. "It's fine. We should hurry, though. The Rogue was supposed to be at Northsbury in two days.

If we don't ride faster, he will kill the king and leave before we ever get there."

Jade nodded her agreement and urged her horse into a brisk canter, allowing Aston to move ahead of her and lead the way.

**

As night fell, Aston was forced to slow down. He couldn't see where he was going anymore, and his knight's training didn't help this far from Fridel. It had been almost a year since he'd been to Northsbury. He'd gone with Talbot and King Donn the winter before for the king's winter ball. The path was unfamiliar, and, for the second time since his death sentence, he found himself afraid.

"Is something wrong, Aston?" Jade asked, bringing her horse up beside Sterling. She gazed around at the surrounding trees.

"I've only been to Northsbury once, and it was always daylight when we were travelling. We can't stop here, though. If we don't make it there by tomorrow evening, we will be too late to save the king."

"Do you really care about the king's life, or do you just want to catch the Rogue?" Jade asked him.

Aston whipped his head to the side, narrowing his eyes. "I may be a wanted man, Jade, but I'm still a knight at heart. Saving the lives of innocent people will always come before my own gain."

Jade nodded and turned away from his piercing gaze. "If you go with what the Rogue says, the men he kills aren't exactly innocent."

"Are you condoning killing these people?" Aston asked, reining Sterling in and turning in his saddle.

Jade stopped as well but didn't turn to face Aston. "I'm not saying it's right, what he's doing. I'm just stating an opinion," she explained, slowly urging her horse forward again.

Aston was forced to follow. "To answer your question, yes, I do care about the king's life. More than my own. You have to care more about the lives of other people to be a knight. That's not saying that finding the Rogue isn't just as important to me, but if I can stop it, I won't allow the king to die." Jade nodded, seemingly convinced. "We can go faster now. This road leads to King Roland's castle," Aston added, looking down. Jade followed his gaze, noticing they were on a well-traveled dirt road.

As they quickened their pace, Jade glanced sideways at Aston. She sent a prayer upwards, though she wasn't quite sure what to pray for. Should she pray they would arrive in time to stop the Rogue and capture him? Should she pray they arrived too late and the Rogue would already be gone? Aston and the Rogue were both people she cared deeply about; she didn't want either of them to be hurt.

With a jolt, Jade realized that she couldn't keep her promise to Richie. She wanted to help Aston clear his name, but she couldn't condemn Ernst in his place. She cursed under her breath, fighting the tears welling behind her eyes. She was going to have to choose between Ernst and Aston. After knowing Aston for just a couple of days, she found her choice was becoming harder to make.

**

Jade startled awake, quickly realizing that they had stopped and Aston's hand was on her shoulder. "Are we there?" she asked, sitting up and rubbing her eyes. Aston had allowed her to sleep the night before, saying they would be in Northsbury soon enough and that they could slow down.

"Yes, Jade. Welcome to Northsbury," he said, gesturing ahead of them. Jade followed his movement, and her eyes widened as she took in the city. She'd traveled to Duke Roland's every year with her family in the winter, but she never paid much attention to the city. She spent the ride there in a carriage, her nose stuck in a book.

She'd never realized before how beautiful the city was. Where Adion was broken stone streets and drooping trees, Northsbury had streets made of cobblestone and tall, elegant, blossoming shrubs. As they made their way down the street, Jade took in the well-maintained buildings, the smiling citizens, and the flowers blooming in wooden boxes on every window sill. Aston looked a bit uncomfortable, walking in the middle of the day through town, but no one spared him a passing glance.

"I suppose news travels slowly from Fridel to Northsbury. No one seems to know who I am," Aston said, turning to look at Jade.

"What does that mean for us?" Jade asked him.

Aston smiled, jumping down from Sterling. "It means we can stay here," he said, motioning to the building they'd stopped in front of.

Jade looked up and smiled, her eyes crinkling. "Really? We can stay here?" she exclaimed, bouncing slightly in her saddle. When Aston nodded, she laughed and jumped down from Edward, pulling Aston into a hug before going inside.

Aston looked up again, his eyes glancing at the sign. The triangular board depicted the silhouette of a knight on a horse, a plume rising from his helmet: Knight's Inn. It was fitting, he thought. He handed Sterling and Edward over to the inn's stable hand and followed Jade inside. He was surprised he didn't find her in the main room.

Aston walked to the desk at the front of the inn, clearing his throat to get the innkeeper's attention. When she looked up at him, she immediately stopped what she was doing and leaned forward, exposing a good amount of her chest for his eyes.

"I was wondering where the young woman who just walked in went," Aston said, deciding to get right to the point.

The woman frowned and straightened, crossing her arms over her chest. "Upstairs, third room on the right," she said, looking down at her desk.

Aston pulled his coin purse from his pocket and opened it. "How much for the room?" he asked.

The lady waved him off. "It's been taken care of."

Aston frowned as he put his purse away before heading up the stairs. He found the third one and knocked, not wanting to intrude on Jade.

"Come in," she called.

Aston stepped inside and smiled. Jade was lying on the only bed in the room, her arms crossed behind her head, her legs taking up most of the rest. She pulled her legs together when he walked in and patted the empty side of the bed beside her.

Confused, Aston walked over and sat beside Jade, glancing around the room. A tall wardrobe occupied one corner, and there was a single window overlooking the town with thread-bare brown curtains. Aside from that, the bed was the only other furniture in the room.

"Well, lay down. Get some sleep," Jade ordered, interrupting his thoughts. She folded her arms back under her head and closed her eyes.

"This isn't proper," Aston said, uncomfortable. He cleared his throat and looked away from the princess, folding his hands in his lap and squirming.

"Well, I didn't think to get two rooms. I thought it would be pointless. Besides, if you are going to be my protector, you need to be in the same room as me," Jade stated, opening her eyes again and looking over at Aston.

Aston looked down at her and sighed, giving in and laying down beside her. "How did you pay for this room, anyway?" Aston asked.

Jade cringed. "I 'borrowed' some money from my parents when I left," she answered.

Aston laughed and turned onto his side, facing the wall away from Jade. He felt Jade turn around as well. Aston didn't intend to sleep. He didn't want to fall asleep and not wake up in time to catch the Rogue. The knight didn't want to have to go back to Fridel. By now, everyone would know what he had done, and the price on his head would be high.

He heard Jade's slow breathing and knew she'd fallen asleep. He got up slowly, careful not to jar the bed and wake her. He left the room, locking the door behind him, and went downstairs, going to the stable to grab their bags. When he reached the room again, Aston remembered the letter Richie had given him from King Aric. Curious, he dug the letter from the pack and went downstairs to read it.

Donn,

I appreciate the help you sent. Prince Talbot held everyone together when The Rogue Royal got away. You should know I don't blame your knight or your son for what happened to Duke Aeron. If Aston and Talbot had not been there, we wouldn't have found The Duke when we did, and my daughter might be dead as well. I want you to thank Talbot for staying with her while Aston went after the Rogue. She is a fragile soul, so like her mother.

That said, I have news of her. My daughter has run away. I haven't seen my son in a month and now she is gone as well. I don't know where I am failing as a fathe,r but I fear she was angry with me. I had arranged for Duke Aeron's eldest son, Marquess Jacob, to marry her, but my daughter is spirited.

If you could send someone to help me find her, I would be most grateful. Maybe Aston? I have heard he is the best of your knights, and I believe he would be able to coax her into returning home. I hope for word from you soon.

Your friend,

Aric

Aston raised a brow at the letter. King Aric had wanted him to come and find his daughter? He wondered what Donn's reply would have been. I'm sorry, I can't send Aston because I hanged him? Rereading the letter, Aston found what he needed.

"I want you to thank Talbot for staying with her while Aston went after The Rogue... King Aric knows it was Talbot that stayed with the princess, and not me," he whispered, reading the line again. This letter could be the key to his salvation.

With a sigh, he placed the letter aside. If he returned with the letter, King Donn would think it was forged. He would accuse Aston of stealing the real letter and forging a new one and he would be in worse shape than he was already.

Aston jumped as he felt small hands on his shoulders, his body tensing as he was pulled from his thoughts. Grabbing the dagger at his belt, he tilted his head back and looked up, finding Jade standing over him. He let out the breath he had been holding and released his dagger, relaxing. "Jade," he said, acknowledging her presence.

She smiled at him but quickly dropped the expression. "What are you doing down here? You should be sleeping," she stated, letting go of his shoulders and coming around to sit beside him on the hard sofa.

Aston laughed halfheartedly. "I found something that could clear my name," he said, tossing the letter onto Jade's lap.

Jade picked up the letter carefully. After reading it, she raised an eyebrow and looked at him. "You're on first name basis with...King Aric?" She'd paused to read the signature.

Aston shrugged. "He's always been kind to me when my travels take me to Adion," he explained.

Jade nodded. "How could this save you?" she asked. Aston pointed to the letter and she gasped. "Aric knew you went after the Rogue?" she asked. "This is great!"

The knight shook his head. "King Donn would claim the letter was a forgery if I brought it to him. This doesn't change anything. I might have King Aric on my side, but, if I show up in Adion, I don't know *what* would happen to me. I'd probably be thrown in the dungeon and left until King Donn arrived."

"Oh…I'm sorry," Jade said, refolding the letter so that the address was on the outside. She returned the letter to Aston's lap and stood. "If you aren't going to sleep, we might as well go and see the town," she offered, holding a hand out towards him.

Aston stared at her hand for a moment, contemplating. On the ride into town, no one had recognized him, but that didn't mean that they wouldn't. Was it really a good idea, going into the market in the middle of the afternoon? The look on Jade's face, the blatant excitement, made him sigh. He accepted the hand she offered, allowing Jade to pull him to his feet.

Once standing, Jade smiled and pulled him out the door, leading him onto the streets of Northsbury. The air was thick with the smells of winter. Baking apple pies, the faint smell of pine, and cinnamon filled Aston's nose, and he breathed deeply. Winter was almost there; another week and snow would start falling, blanketing the ground in its soft, white powder. When winter came, he would have to find a place to stay with Jade. He couldn't allow her to live in the forest, sleeping on the frozen ground. Aston made a note to talk to Delgrab about finding a small cabin for him to use for the winter.

Jade's eyes lit up as she walked through Summerslade. The streets were alive with jesters, musicians, and merchants. Stalls lined the streets selling jewelry, cloth, pottery, and ribbons. Store owners were outside with trays of their products to sell, competing with the travelling merchants who had stopped before the Winter Ball. Several people stopped Jade as they walked the street, offering her jewelry and samples of fresh fruit, but Aston made sure not to let her talk to too many people.

Aston was grateful the king's soldiers seemed to be absent from the market. Undoubtedly, they were all at the palace, being briefed on what to do in case the Rogue showed up. Which he would. Right now, it was more important that the king's life be protected than that his people were behaving during their winter festival. Jade, however, seemed to be enjoying herself. He bought her an apple covered in a sweet, sticky candy and laughed as she attempted to eat it without getting completely filthy. And she insisted they stop at every vendor to look and marvel at what they were selling.

As they traveled through the village, Aston couldn't help but keep his eyes out for Talbot. The prince was the one person that could ruin this mission for him. If Talbot found him, he had no question that the prince would try to stop him. He couldn't afford to be stopped now, not when he was so close. If he couldn't catch the Rogue here, in Northsbury, he feared he wouldn't get another chance.

"It's especially difficult when siblings leave the nest and grow into their own person, often apart from other siblings and parents. The ones we shared so much with growing up, we suddenly have nothing in common with, it seems."
-Unknown Author -

Thirteen

Jacob frowned. It had been five days since he reached Adion and he still had not seen his bride. He sat in the king's throne, tossing a gold coin in the air and catching it, one handed. He'd spent the last five days wallowing around the castle, giving the servants a hard time and harassing the cooks. King Aric had finally sent him to the throne room, promising Jade would be along any time.

He knew it was all rubbish. The princess hadn't been in the palace since he'd arrived, he was sure. He'd snuck to her room several times and nothing ever changed. Her mirror was tilted just so, her wardrobe slightly open, her bed neatly made. No one had entered that room.

Standing, Jacob left the throne room in favor of something more interesting. As he passed the library, he paused, hearing King Aric and his wife talking on the other side of the door.

"We have to tell him something, dearest. We can't just let him wonder about the palace until Jade decides to come home," Queen Margaret was saying.

Jacob heard King Aric sigh. "I know, Margaret. What do we tell the boy? Jade knew she would have to marry you and ran away? Jade wanted love and not duty?"

The marquess reared back, scowling at the door. Who would run away from him? What kind of foolish princess had they raised in Adion?

"We have to be discreet, Aric. If we told Jacob the true reason our daughter left, their marriage would never be saved, and our contract with Summerslade would be broken. She's a smart young woman, Aric. You'd do well to remember that."

"I know, I know. But she's never been rebellious before this. She's always seemed generally interested in being Queen one day," Aric said.

"Yes, dear, *Queen*. Not Duchess of Summerslade. She wants to be Queen of Adion. You must have realized that?" Margaret chastised.

Jacob had heard enough. His bride had run away from him? Was his family not good enough? He came from a noble line, but it wasn't enough for his Jade. No, she had to run off and find adventure, romance! Jacob stormed down the hallway, knocking over a young girl carrying clean towels as he raced for his room.

The duke's son grabbed his satchel and stuffed it with half the clothes he had brought with him. He made his way to the kitchen and grabbed two loaves of bread and a block of cheese before leaving the palace and heading toward the stables. His horse was in a stall at the back of the stable. Jacob wasted no time in saddling the animal, showing a halter into his pack as well.

If Jade wanted to find adventures, she could find them with *him*.

**

Aston pushed Jade behind him. Night had fallen and they were outside the palace, standing alone on the edge of the stone path leading to the castle doors. They were just outside the ring of light offered by the tall torches lining the path, and Jade had been about to stride forward into the light. Aston took a deep breath, trying to calm his nerves.

Jade had had the bright idea that they should enter the castle instead of waiting outside, as that hadn't worked so well for Aston the last time. The knight, on the other hand, didn't want to get anywhere near the inside of the castle, unless he had to.

"No one has recognized you, Aston! You're safe here," Jade placated, patting him on the back.

"Just because commoners don't know who I am *doesn't* mean the king won't," he replied. He looked up at the palace before him again. Dark grey stone covered in moss, and about two hundred people inside who would want to bring him right back to Fridel to claim the prize on his head.

"Calm down and follow me. No one will notice you, I promise," she encouraged, gliding forward from the shadows. Aston made a grab for her, missed, and gave up, following her with a gentle curse along the stone path leading to the front door. He tried his best to look inconspicuous, but more than once he caught himself staring at the ground or fiddling with his sword's bronze hilt. He was uncomfortable, but Jade glided before him like a true lady.

She'd changed before they left the inn, pulling a dress from her bag and walking down the hall to the bath area. When she'd come back, Aston had stared at her until she walked out the door, expecting him to follow. Now, walking behind her, he caught himself staring again.

Jade's dress was baby blue, long and flowing. White lace wrapped around each sleeve, which cut off at her elbows. The same elegant material wrapped around the collar, which dipped low on her neck, allowing just a peek of the pale flesh underneath. Every once in a while, with her flouncing steps, Aston caught a glimpse of the riding boots she still wore. He smiled. His Jade was a warrior, all business when needed.

His eyes widened at the thought. His Jade? When had she become *his* Jade?

As if hearing her name in his head, Jade turned and gave him a dazzling smile. She'd lined her eyes again and somehow managed to do her hair without any tools. She'd pulled some of it back and fastened it at the back of her head with a little silver clip, allowing the rest to wave over her shoulders and down her back. She looked more like a princess than ever before, and Aston found himself wondering who she really was.

As they neared the front door, the guards stepped in front of them.

"Halt, who goes there?" the taller of the two asked.

Aston froze, not sure what to answer.

Thankfully, Jade spoke. "I am Princess Jade du Halen. King Aric du Halen sent me with one of our knights to protect your king."

Aston gaped at Jade. Jade du Halen? *The* Jade du Halen? The runaway princess King Aric wanted him to track had been with him the entire time? He closed his mouth with an audible click when the guards cast him a funny look, remembering that this wasn't supposed to be news to him.

Jade grabbed a charm hanging from the thin silver chain at her neck and lifted it over her head, sliding the necklace off. She held it out for the guards to see. The man who had spoken nodded his approval, seeing King Aric's crest engraved onto the large emerald charm. After exchanging one last glance, the guards moved aside and bowed, allowing them entrance.

As soon as the guards were out of sight and they were alone in the hall, Aston grabbed Jade by the elbow, spun her around, and pushed her into a wall. "Why didn't you tell me who you were?" he growled, his voice low and angry.

Jade swallowed, paling a bit. "I didn't want you to send me home," she replied, her voice small.

Aston cursed and released her, turning away and running a hand through his dusty hair. "Do you have *any* idea what would happen to me if people saw us together? People who knew you were missing?" Aston started pacing as his mind whirled through the possibilities.

"I would tell them I ran away from Marquess Jacob," Jade replied, standing tall.

"That's what this is about? You ran away because you didn't want to get *married*?" Aston asked, turning back to her and pressing her against the wall again. "Are you *daft*, woman?"

His voice rose when he insulted her, and Aston watched as Jade's eyes flashed with her anger.

"I am not *daft*, Aston Smith. I am a young woman who doesn't want to marry a stuck up little boy," she answered.

"Jacob of Summerslade is older than you," came his reply.

"In age maybe, but not in mind, soul, or *spirit*. He acts like a toddler, Aston! He throws tantrums to get what he wants! He missed his own father's funeral to come to Adion to marry me! Who would want to marry a man like that?" Jade exclaimed, putting her hands on Aston's shoulders and forcing him back a few steps. She released him as soon as she had room to step away from the wall and clenched her fists at her sides.

"Every woman who doesn't have the privilege to marry into the royal family," Aston responded sarcastically. He wasn't sure if he was angrier about Jade being who she was or at the thought of her marrying Marquess Jacob.

"Well, they can have him. In case you haven't noticed, I already *am* in the royal family. Therefore, I don't need Jacob." Her thoughts voiced, Jade walked away, leaving Aston to run after her. But Aston wasn't finished with their conversation, so he fell into step beside her and spoke out of the corner of his mouth.

"Are there any other secrets you feel like sharing?" Aston whispered as they made their way down a well-lit corridor. Servants and guards were scattered through this one, some whispering, some talking in normal voices, all somber. Normally at this time, the servants were already decorating for the winter ball. This year, every eye was open, looking for someone suspicious. Their king was in danger; no one felt the need for celebration.

"Why don't you go and talk to someone, see if anyone has noticed anything suspicious," Jade ordered Aston. At his raised brow, she rolled her eyes and shoved him away. "Say you are on official business for King Aric du Halen and no one will question you," she said.

The knight sighed and walked away, shaking his head as he realized Jade wouldn't answer any more of his questions right now. He approached a group of servants standing not too far from them.

**

Jade waited until he seemed deep in conversation before she left, making her way toward the throne room. Ernst was probably already in the castle somewhere; she would answer Aston's questions for later. Right now, finding The Rogue Royal before he killed King Roland was more important.

Several courtiers stopped her to exchange pleasantries on her way, but Jade made her exchanges and then quickly excused herself. When she reached the throne room, she was surprised to see no guards posted outside. When she entered, the king was alone.

"Sire?" she inquired.

The king looked up at her, his eyes swollen and red. "Oh, Lady Jade. What an unexpected pleasure," he said, standing and bringing the young woman into a hug.

"What are you doing in here alone, Your Majesty?" Jade asked, allowing the king to resume his seat while she settled herself comfortably on the floor at his feet, her back to the door. She'd never been a fan of protocol, and in the king's last hour she wanted him to be comfortable.

"It doesn't matter how many guards one has. This *Rogue Royal* always sends notice about when and where he is going to kill, and he always succeeds. I don't want to fight my fate. If he didn't think I deserved to die, he wouldn't be after me," the king said, his eyes shining with tears. "I have done horrible things, Lady du Halen. Things I should not speak of with someone so innocent."

"Sire," Jade replied softly, feeling tears in her eyes as well. She wasn't as close to King Roland as she was to many others, but he always invited her family for his winter ball. She'd spent every winter, as long as she could remember, coming to his palace dressed in her best dress, dancing the night away with her father and any young man who wanted her. This palace was as familiar to her as her own.

"It's alright, Lady du Halen. I am not afraid of death," he consoled, glancing up as the doors opened again. Jade knew without looking who it would be. The clock in the hall began to chime; midnight. Time for the Rogue to kill his target.

"Why are you here, Jade?"

She heard his deep voice right behind her. She hadn't realized he'd gotten so close. "You've become quieter, Ernst," she replied, not turning around to meet his gaze. She knew what she would see; cold, steely emerald eyes, so much like her own.

"You've become naïve, sister."

"Pain is inevitable. Suffering is optional."
-M. Kathleen Casey -

Fourteen

What happened to you, Ernst?" Jade asked, her eyes fixed on the king. He sat, unmoving, in his throne, his eyes studying the face of the man about to murder him.

"I grew up, Jay. I left the palace and learned things no man should know. Now, I am righting other's wrongs with my own."

"You don't have to kill anyone else, Ernst. Go home. Go home to Mother, and Father. Tell them you love them, and you're sorry you left. Your secret will be safe," Jade pleaded. It was the same conversation she'd had with him in Adion. He'd killed Duke Aeron across the hall from her bedroom. She'd tried to stop him, but he was stronger than her.

"You know I can't do that, baby sister. These men *deserve* what they get." Ernst was standing beside her, now, and Jade looked up, surprised to see he was wearing a cobalt mask. She could still tell it was him, but she doubted anyone else would be able to.

She stood, putting herself between her brother and the king. "I can't let you do this, Ernst," she said, backing up until the backs of her knees were even with the king's.

"You can't stop me. Didn't you learn that last time, before you squealed like a girl and called Prince Talbot to your side?"

Jade scrunched her nose at her brother. "I didn't know Prince Talbot was there any more than you did, brother. Why King Donn would send his son, I don't know, but I *didn't* know the prince was in the palace. I thought you were going to kill me, Ernst. That's the *only* reason I screamed. I would never do anything to make you unsafe! You should know that," Jade said, begging her brother to understand. She knew that if he was set on killing the king, the king would die. She wished the monarch would stand, run, do *something* other than wait for death.

"I'm sure you didn't, Jade. However, you almost got me caught. I won't allow that again," Ernst threatened, narrowing his emerald eyes. He took another step closer to Jade, and she leaned back, placing her hands on the arms of the throne behind her. She put a defiant look on her face, daring him to hurt her. He was her brother; he cared about her. Right?

Ernst pulled his ruby hilted dagger from his belt and held it up for her to see. "This won't go through both of you," he said. "Your choice, Jade. Save the king there, that's already given up on life, or save that knight who you've been following around."

Jade went from terrified to angry, and she felt her cheeks reddening as anger flared through her. "What did you do to him?" she asked, taking her arms from the throne and standing tall again. She took a step toward her brother, but stopped when he turned the dagger on her.

"He got in my way, Jay. That knight almost captured me in Adion. You're lucky I didn't run him through where he stood. I know how much he means to you, so I left him alive," he answered.

Jade paled and looked out the door. She hadn't realized it before, but Aston should have been in there. He wouldn't have wasted so much time talking to servants; he would have followed her and run in when the clock struck midnight.

"Ernst, please," she tried one last time. When her brother didn't back down, Jade turned to the king sitting silently behind her. "I apologize," she said quietly, bending down to kiss the king on the cheek. He didn't react, but she hadn't really expected him to. The king was already dead on the inside.

Jade took one last look at her brother before racing from the hall, making her way through the palace, back to where she'd left Aston. She heard the sound of metal piercing flesh, the scream the king let out as his blood was released, but she ignored the sounds.

The princess felt guilty, leaving the king to die, but she couldn't let Ernst kill Aston instead. Aston wasn't ready to give up on life, and it wasn't her call to decide his fate.

She found him laid out in the middle of the hall. Jade rushed to the knight, sliding to the ground beside him and pulling his head into her lap. She tried not to notice the blood she was sitting in and instead went to work checking him over. A long wound stretching from his shoulder to his collar bone on his left arm seemed to be the cause of the blood. A bump on his right temple was the reason he was unconscious.

"Aston? Aston?" she whispered, shaking her knight, fearing the worst. He groaned, but didn't wake up. Looking around herself, Jade cringed and forced down her want to heave; the hall looked like a war zone. Several of the king's soldiers had fought, despite their king's orders not to. The men who had tried to stand up to Ernst were dead; all except for Aston, who he'd kept alive for her.

Somewhere, deep inside the murderer, her brother still lived.

**

Aston woke up confused. His arm and chest hurt, his head was throbbing and he had no idea where he was. As his memories came flooding back, he sprang up in his bed, automatically falling back again as the world tilted sideways.

"Aston!" he heard a female voice cry.

Turning his head to the side, he saw that Jade was there. Taking a closer look, he realized two things: he was back in the inn, and Jade had been crying. "What happened?" he asked, frowning at his voice. Had it always been so deep and crackly? Jade helped him sit up and handed him a glass of water, which he drank greedily. "What happened?" he tried again, pleased when his voice came out fairly normal.

"You fought the Rogue," Jade explained.

Aston nodded; that part he remembered. He remembered seeing a masked man walking down the hall and thinking that *definitely* counted as suspicious. He remembered drawing his sword and charging the man, remembered the Rogue crouching low, grabbing his dagger, and pulling it across his chest. "How did I get here? What happened to King Roland?"

Jade looked away, standing and going to the window. She pulled the curtains aside and looked down at the street below. "A few soldiers from the palace helped me bring you here. The king is dead," she answered, keeping her eyes averted.

"He was so fast, Jade." Jade turned, meeting his eyes. "I've never fought anyone who moved like that. He was under me with his blade in me before I even had time to bring my sword up." The knight turned away, staring at a spot on the wall.

Jade sighed and let the curtains fall back over the window, casting the room in shadow. She walked to the bed and sat down beside Aston, careful not to jar him. "He's a practiced murderer, Aston. How many palaces do you think he's snuck into? How many guards do you think he's killed?" Jade asked, and Aston knew she was trying to make him feel better.

"Why did he leave me alive?" Aston asked. Jade met his gaze, but said nothing. "All those other soldiers, in the hall with me. He killed them without a second glance. But me...he left *me* alive."

"Maybe he thought your wound would kill you," Jade offered, but Aston shook his head.

"He would have known better. Something made him spare me. We need to find where he's going next." At Aston's words, something crashed through the window, causing him to throw his arms around Jade and shield her with his body. He cursed; how could he have gotten Jade into a life so dangerous?

When nothing else happened, he slowly moved, allowing Jade to sit up again. She looked at the floor beside them and bent down, picking a brick up off the floor. A thick piece of paper was connected to it by a thick rope. Aston took the brick from Jade and tore the rope off before quickly unfolding the thick parchment.

Your prince is next, Aston of Fridel.

One single line, but it told Aston everything he needed to know.

**

Talbot sulked the entire ride home. The king had been murdered, he hadn't seen Aston, and Ernst was nowhere to be found. He blamed the men behind him for missing the fight. Half of his army had gone in to fight off the Rogue, leaving Talbot outside with the other half. He'd tried to go in, but the men had restrained him, saying the murderer would kill him as soon as he met him.

The half of his army that had disappeared inside the palace had never come out. They'd been slaughtered, and Talbot was almost grateful they hadn't let him inside. Almost. He was still angry enough at having missed Aston that he wasn't ready to forgive anyone just yet.

"Ok, we can rest here for a minute," Talbot announced, guiding Red off the dirt road and into the shade of the trees. His horse seemed grateful for the reprieve from the heat; the prince was happy to get out of the sun as well.

He watched what was left of his army gather under the shade, feeling restless. He'd brought his father's best knights with him and The Rogue Royal hadn't even been bothered by them. He had been thinking a lot about what Ernst had told him, and he feared the prince might be right. What if the Rogue did come after him? Talbot wasn't the fairest prince, especially with what he'd done to Aston.

He'd ruined a knight's life just to keep himself from a scolding and a slap on the writst.

Talbot cursed under his breath; he *was* a perfect target for the Rogue. "Ok, men, enough rest! Time to get going. We can rest once the sun goes down. For now, we push toward Fridel!" His terror reigning foremost in his mind, Talbot intended to push his men as far as he could that day. He knew he wouldn't feel safe again until he was back in the palace.

He wasn't even sure he would feel safe *then*.

**

"You can't go back to Fridel, Aston! It's a suicide mission!" Jade said, scrambling around the room after him. She'd been trying to get him to go back to bed since he'd read the note, but he was determined to leave.

"I can't let Talbot die, either, now can I?" Aston asked, grimacing. His wound hurt more when he was moving then he'd expected it to.

"Why not?" Jade asked, throwing her arms in the air. Aston turned to look at her. "Talbot is the reason you're here, Aston, bleeding and hurting."

"No, Jade, the Rogue is the reason I'm bleeding and hurting. Not only because he hurt me," he added when he saw Jade open her mouth to speak, "but because if he hadn't been killing people, I wouldn't have had a reason to be with Talbot in Adion that night."

Jade shut her mouth, as if realizing he was right. Instead, she focused her energy on helping him pack. "He didn't set a date, Aston. That means he isn't going after him right away." Aston looked over at her, his expression hard. "He *always* sets a date. Relax, gain your strength back, and *then* we will go to Fridel. Together," she said.

Aston studied the princess a moment longer, wondering if she was just trying to stall him. He realized she was right, of course. The Rogue always said exactly when he would kill his target. The note he'd received, however, only told him that Talbot would be targeted, not when.

With a sigh, Aston sat on the bed, carefully laying himself down. He hissed in pain as his shoulder moved and Jade was at his side in an instant, lowering him onto the mattress. He smiled up at her, trying to remove her frown. He didn't want her worrying about him.

"I'm fine, Jade," he said.

She shook her head at him. "You always say that," she replied. Aston looked at her, expecting her to say more. "You told Richie you were fine when he found you in the clearing. You tell Delgrab and Alys not to worry about you. And now, when you're hurt, you're telling me you're okay?" Jade didn't mean for the last part to come out as a question but it did.

"I *am* okay. I'm hurt, yes, but I'm alive. Wounds heal, Jade. Only lost lives can't be restored." Jade nodded and turned away. "Why do you care so much, anyway? I'm just your bodyguard," Aston said.

Jade sniffed and he realized she was crying. "I don't understand this, Aston, but you are more to me than that. When I first found you, in the woods, you looked so strong and proud. When I learned your story, I didn't understand how anyone could still be so calm. I would have been jumping off a bridge or riding my horse through a battle. I didn't understand how you kept it all together and managed to put up with me at the same time."

"Jade," Aston began, but she stopped him.

"I can't explain it, can't tell you why, but I don't want you to go after the Rogue. Find another way to prove you're innocent. Use me, if you have to, but don't go after him."

"Use you? Use you how?" Aston asked, struggling to sit up again.

Jade helped him before she answered. "*I'm* the woman who screamed, Aston. I'm the one Talbot rushed in to save, the one who allowed the Rogue to get away from you."

Aston's eyes widened. He hadn't thought about that. "You could prove I wasn't the one checking on the woman," he said. Jade nodded. "You know Talbot came into your room. You never saw me there," he continued. Another nod from the princess. "It still wouldn't be enough," he said, slumping.

"Why not? Is the word of a princess not good enough?"

"Word will get around that you are traveling with me, Jade. They'll think I forced you to say those things to save your own life. They'll think I threatened you," he said somberly.

"That's not right! How can people be so cruel and unforgiving!" Jade exclaimed, standing.

Aston only shrugged in answer, staring at the curtains covering the windows. A cool breeze drifted in through the shattered glass, making Aston shiver even though he was covered in a thick wool blanket. "I still need him, Jade. I don't know that he will help me get my old life back, but I'll feel better knowing that the man who ruined it has suffered the same fate as I have."

"What fate, Aston?" Jade asked. "Once he's turned in, he'll be *hanged*," she said, her voice cracking on the last word. She didn't want to think of her brother that way.

"And so will I," Aston replied quietly. "I'll turn him in. I'll be praised for catching him, but it won't be enough for King Donn to drop his sentence. I'll hang with him."

"No. No! I won't let that happen," Jade said. She returned to her spot next to the knight, putting an arm across his shoulders and gently pulling him to her. She took his chin in one hand and forced him to look at her. She almost lost her train of thought as emerald met the ocean, but she pulled herself together. "Why don't you both live?" she asked.

Aston tried to shake his head, but seeing as his chin was captive, the move was futile. Instead, he said, "It's against my code to let a murderer walk free, Jade. A knight's honor doesn't allow it."

"Not even as a personal favor? For a princess?"

"No, Jade, not even for that," Aston sighed, closing his eyes.

He opened them again when he felt a pair of soft lips against his own. Jade's eyes were closed, her hand still resting lightly on his chin. The other arm had moved from his shoulder and was searching the bed beside them. He took her hand, instinctively knowing that was what she desired, and closed his eyes, letting himself fall into this one kiss. After this, he'd have to keep his distance from the princess, but he would allow himself what he wanted this one time.

The knight pushed against her lips, returning the kiss she gave him. He didn't push it any farther than simply lips touching; he didn't need to get himself in any deeper with the Princess of Adion than he already had. Aston pulled away shortly after the thought entered his head, watching as Jade's eyes slowly opened.

"There's no harm in trying, right?" she asked. Jade stood and left the room, saying something about finding ice for his wound. Aston found himself wondering if she was talking about the favor she'd asked, or the kiss.

Had she kissed him to see if he'd bend?

> *"To love means loving the unlovable.*
> *To forgive means pardoning the*
> *unpardonable. Faith means believing the*
> *unbelievable. Hope means hoping when*
> *everything seems hopeless."*
> - G. K. Chesterton -

Fifteen

Jacob slowed his horse to a walk as the gates of Fridel came into view. He'd heard from a servant that Aston Smith was sent to look for Jade. He thought the King of Fridel might be able to tell him where Aston went.

As soon as he identified himself to the guards, Jacob's horse was taken to the stables to be rested. He was sent to the palace and directed to the throne room. As he walked the halls, he caught people sending him sideways glances, but no one talked to him.

King Donn was seated on his throne when Jacob entered the room. He walked briskly down the red carpet, stopping in front of the middle throne and going down on one knee. He bowed his head and waited for King Donn to acknowledge him.

"Marquess Jacob. Welcome to my home," King Donn said. Jacob stood and nodded in thanks.

"I am here on orders from King Aric. I was told you sent Aston Smith to search for Jade du Halen," he lied. King Donn's eyes widened.

"Where did that information come from?" he asked Jacob, his voice frantic.

"From King Aric. He sent you a letter," Jacob said, his brow furrowing in confusion. Did King Donn not send Aston, after all?

"Aston Smith is a *traitor* to Fridel. He was present in Adion the night your father was killed," King Donn said coldly.

"He was there?" Jacob murmured. The king nodded. "Why would King Aric send for him?"

"Aric likely doesn't know that Aston betrayed us that night. You should return to Adion. Send Aric word that he won't find his daughter, or Aston Smith, here."

Jacob nodded before turning and leaving the throne room. Aston Smith, a traitor? Surely King Aric would not send a traitor to find his daughter? He would send a man he trusted.

King Donn must be wrong about Aston, Jacob thought, returning to the stables. He ordered the stable hand to prepare his horse before mounting and riding from the stables. He wasn't sure where he was going. A small voice behind him stopped him.

"Wait! Wait, sir, wait!" Jacob turned around and frowned at the small redheaded child running towards him.

"What do you want, boy? Identify yourself," he spat. The boy flinched, but didn't back down.

"My name is Richard. I'm a maid," he answered. Jacob laughed.

"A boy maid? Next thing you know, Fridel will have woman stable hands," he joked.

"Aston Smith isn't a traitor. King Donn is wrong," Richie responded, and Jacob immediately stopped laughing.

"Continue, boy. Tell me what you know."

"Talbot and Aston were in Adion when your father was killed, but Aston tried to catch The Rogue while Talbot stayed behind with the princess. If anyone should be called a traitor, it should be Talbot. King Donn won't listen to anyone, though. He believes his son is innocent." Richie looked at his feet, frowning.

"So, Aston *is* innocent. I thought as much." Jacob took a silver coin from his pocket and flipped it into the air. Richie caught the coin in both hands and looked at it, his eyes shining. He looked up at Jacob questioningly.

"For your information, boy. Everyone deserves payment of some sort," Jacob answered. He dug his heels into his steed's sides and the horse raced off, leaving Richie in the dust.

"They're in Northsbury!" Richie called. Jacob waved a hand to let Richie know he had heard him. He turned left out the gate, finally having a destination.

**

"This is frustrating," Aston told Jade. She was sitting on the edge of the bed, reading a book she'd picked up from the local bookshop. She looked at Aston when he spoke, pointing at the line she'd been reading so she wouldn't lose her place.

"Are you hurting?" she asked him, frowning.

Aston shook his head. "Not really. I'm pretty numb. I just hate *sitting* here," he replied.

"You're used to constant travel, no rest. This will be good for you," Jade told him. When he didn't reply, she turned back to her book. Aston sat up and moved forwards, bringing his legs out from under the covers and sliding to the end of the bed. He looked over Jade's shoulder, reading with her as she moved her finger along the page.

"He was a brave man, always fighting. She wanted to tame him. She wanted to take him into her arms and make him feel like he was home," he read aloud.

Jade smiled at him. "This is one of my favorite books. Father bought me a copy when I was young. I read it every winter," she told him. She sighed and closed the book, setting it in her lap.

"Jade, I've been wanting to ask you…"

"About last night?" she finished for him. Aston looked away, but Jade still caught his nod. "I meant it."

Aston turned to Jade. She looked beautiful, sitting in the faint light coming through the curtains. Her auburn hair formed a halo around her face. Her emerald eyes were locked on his. He leaned closer, not closing his eyes, and his heart leapt into his throat when he saw her moving too.

When their lips met, Aston allowed his eyes to close. It was different than the first time. Where that was unexpected and spontaneous, this was planned and simple. Aston leaned even further forward, pushing Jade onto her back and lying on top of her, supporting himself with his elbows. He never allowed their lips to disconnect.

As he deepened the kiss, he felt Jade's hands go to his shoulders. He tried to hold back his small gasp when her hand rested on his wound, but Jade felt him go still. She quickly moved her hands to his stomach and pushed him back, standing and taking several steps away from the bed. Aston breathed heavily as he watched her, wishing she would come back and be beside him again.

"That was foolish," Jade told him, turning around. Her face was flushed, her lips rosy. Her eyes had darkened. "We can't get carried away, Aston. Not while you're hurt."

For the second time since he'd met her, Jade kissed him and walked away.

Aston leaned back on the bed as soon as the door closed behind Jade. He didn't understand anything about this. He'd met plenty of women, women who were quieter and well-behaved. None of them affected him the way Jade did. Her eyes saw right through him. She was the only person, aside from Richie and Delgrab, who was willing to believe that he had a future. He'd known her for a week and already she was closer to him than so many others he'd had in his life for much longer.

Aston found his eyes traveling to the book Jade had left behind. With nothing better to do, he picked it up, turning to the first page.

The night was cold, the air thick with winter. She had lit a fire in the hearth and now lay curled by its warmth, folded in on herself in the midst of a cotton blanket.

**

Jade sat in the inn's front room until the sun disappeared beyond the horizon and the moon took its place. What was this feeling? It was different from anything she'd ever felt before. She put a hand to her lips, remembering the way Aston's had felt against them. She was smiling like a fool, she knew, but she couldn't stop herself.

When did this become more than just needing someone to look after me? When did this knight find a way into my heart? Jade glanced at the stairs. Her knight was up there now, lying in pain from a wound her brother had inflicted.

Her heart sank as she remembered. Nothing could ever happen between her and Aston. If it did, she would be obligated to save him and she couldn't hurt Ernst that way. She realized she was in an insolvable spot. The way she saw it, she had two choices: save her brother, or save her knight.

There was no way for her to do both.

"Not until we are lost do we begin to understand ourselves."

- Henry David Thoreau -

Sixteen

Aston awoke the next morning extremely satisfied. He had spent the night beside Jade, listening to her soft breathing. He wanted more nights like that one, more mornings of waking up beside her. Those days would have to wait. Jade had only paid for two nights; it was time to leave.

"I can pay for another night, Aston. You know I have the money," Jade said. She wanted Aston to rest, not start going after Ernst again so soon.

"We need to return to Delgrab's. I need to know if Richie has heard anything else from King Donn," Aston said.

With a sigh, Jade followed after him as he left the room. He had his bag in one hand and hers in the other. She took hers from the knight, not wanting Aston to strain his arm.

After checking out of their room, Jade and Aston went to the stable. Jade tipped the boy working there to tack their horses while she and Aston waited.

"I really think we should stay one more night. Your Rogue won't go after Talbot without setting a date, Aston."

"You said that already, Jade. I know. I'll feel better knowing I'm closer to him, that's all." Aston looked away, not wanting to discuss any further. He was a knight. He'd spent more nights wounded outside with no bed to lay in than he could count. Jade didn't understand because she'd been brought up in a position where if she was hurt, or sick, she could lay down until she was better. Knights didn't have that option.

Once the horses were ready, Aston wasted no time mounting Sterling and leaving town, Jade close behind him. In two days, they would reach Delgrab's cabin. Aston still intended to ask Del if there was a place he and Jade could spend the winter. He didn't want to drag her around through the snow all season.

Already, the air felt colder. The harsh wind whipped at his cheeks, quickly reddening them. He looked over his shoulder and saw Jade hunched down in her saddle, letting her horse block the wind. Aston smiled. If only the princess knew how ridiculous she looked, her hair blowing everywhere, peeking out from behind her stallion's head. Aston found himself laughing then, his sour mood lifted.

Jade scowled at him. She quickly ducked back behind her horse, not used to the cold wind nipping at her face.

"You'll get used to the wind once your face goes numb," he called back to her.

"I'd rather hide and keep my face *warm*," she replied. Aston stopped Sterling and pulled his satchel onto his lap. Reaching in, he pulled out a thick cloak.

"Wrap this around your shoulders and over your head. It will help," he told Jade, who had stopped Edward beside Sterling. She did as she was told, reveling in the warmth the blanket offered.

"Thank you, Aston," she said, her cheeks rosy. Aston nodded and started forward again, the princess right behind.

**

"Father, we tried!" Talbot exclaimed, wishing his father would look at him. He was currently on the floor at his father's feet. He glanced up, but Donn only looked away, staring past his son.

"I want results, Talbot, not excuses! You brought an entire unit with you and brought back only half of that. What happened?" The king turned his eyes back to Talbot, his grey pupils burning with his fury.

"The Rogue Royal was there, Father. I never saw Aston. He might not have been there after all. I sent half of your men in to get your knight, but none of them came back," Talbot explained. He moved to stand, but Donn pushed him back to the floor with his foot.

"You'll stay down there until I tell you otherwise," he ordered. "What do you expect me to do now, Talbot? Hope that whoever The Rogue goes after next decides to send me a letter asking for help? The only reason I knew about this attack was because King Roland and I were close friends. Now he is dead, too. What's it going to take for you to bring Aston to me?"

"Shouldn't we worry more about the The Rogue Royal targeting one of us?" Talbot asked. Ernst's words were still foremost in his mind. With his father angry at him, Talbot stood no chance against The Rogue should he decide to target him next.

"I don't care who that man kills now, Talbot. My closest friends are all dead. If it weren't for Aston's foolishness, they would both still be alive."

"How could Aston have saved King Roland?" Talbot asked, confusion evident in his voice.

"If he hadn't failed with Duke Aeron, I would have sent him to protect Roland. As it is now, I'm stuck with knights half as strong as him and a dimwitted son to watch over my army," Donn exclaimed. He stood from his throne and strode down the red carpet. At the door, he turned. "You can stay there for now, Talbot."

"Father!" Talbot cried, but Donn did not turn around. His footsteps gradually became softer, and soon Talbot could not hear them at all.

The prince looked around himself. He'd never paid much attention to the throne room; it was always just the room he went to to order people around. Now, he realized it really was beautiful. Tall, marble columns were spaced throughout the room. Each one had the country's roaring lion emblem engraved into it right where the column met the ceiling. The golden thrones were kept polished, gleaming in the light let in through the floor to ceiling windows that took up the entire left wall. Burgundy curtains were pulled to the side and held in place by thick, gold tassels.

For the first time, Talbot realized how lucky he was. He had a father who loved him most of the time. His mother was kind and always put others before herself. He had an army that would put their lives on the line to protect him and a country full of people who knew one day he would rule them and respected him.

What had he been doing with his life?

He looked up as the sound of shuffling feet approached. Turning, he spotted Aston's little servant friend, Richard. The boy glanced at Talbot and bowed slightly before proceeding to the thrones. He carried a bucket that was sloshing with soapy water in both hands, a towel clutched tightly between the handle and his palms.

Without looking at Talbot again, the boy began to clean the thrones. He started on the king's, making sure to get every inch gleaming in the late morning sun. When he was finished with King Donn's, he moved on to the queen's. Talbot continued to watch the boy, and Richie sent sideways glances at the prince every once in a while. Finally, the boy stopped what he was doing and turned to face Talbot.

"Is something wrong, Your Highness?"

"Nothing. Just a conversation I had with someone recently." Thinking over the idea, Talbot decided to test his theory on Richie. "Can I ask you something?" he asked the boy.

Richie shrugged. "I suppose so."

"Do you think The Rogue Royal would ever think to come after me?" Talbot asked.

Richie's eyes widened in surprise. "Where did you get that idea, Your Highness?" he asked.

The prince sighed. "It's nothing. Just something I'd been thinking about. Run along. Go…clean something," Talbot ordered. He stood, despite his father's orders, and left the throne room.

**

Richie shrugged and turned back to Talbot's throne, remembering the dream he'd had the night before. Talbot had been sleeping, and The Rogue Royal was standing by his bedside, dagger in hand. He wondered if that had anything to do with the prince's sudden burst of kindness. As he finished washing the prince's throne, he noticed a letter sitting on the floor by the king's. He looked toward the door to make sure Talbot really was gone before picking up the letter. It took him a while, but with Aston's reading lessons, he was able to struggle through the letter.

Donn,

I thought I should let you know that I received word from The Rogue Royal today. He says he sent word to every kingdom, letting them know their royalty was safe until winter is through. I suppose even blood thirsty murders don't like to travel in the winter.

I also received word from the Queen of Northsbury. She says the death of her husband will not put plans for the winter ball on hold. She says her husband would be dishonored if they did not celebrate as usual.

I suppose I will be seeing you and Talbot there next month.

Any news from Aston about my dear daughter?

Your friend,

Aric

Richie didn't understand what most of the letter was about, but one thing did stand out to him. The Rogue wouldn't be killing anyone else until after the snow left.

Smiling, Richie left the room and went to the stables, talking to Vernon for a bit before climbing on Vernon's old mare and leaving the palace. If there was one place Aston would always go back to, it was Delgrab's cabin. If he hurried, Richie could make it there and back before dark. He would leave the letter with Delgrab and hope Aston made it back before the first snow.

**

Night found Aston and Jade halfway home. It also found them camping out in the middle of the forest, winter upon them.

The first flakes of snow had fallen right as the sun was setting, and Aston had quickened their pace, hoping they would be able to reach Delgrab's cabin the next day before the snow started to stick.

As the sun finished its descent, Aston forced Sterling into the forest and off the main road. He wanted to be able to build a fire without worrying about someone seeing it.

"Stay under that blanket until I get this fire started. Stay by Edward. You can share his body heat until I'm done."

Jade nodded, and Aston noticed her teeth were chattering. He worked faster, knowing the princess wouldn't be used to the cold. It took him only a moment to create enough friction to start a fire. He put the flint back in his satchel before grabbing Jade's hand, pulling her close to the fire. He'd taken his own blanket and draped it across the ground; as long as it didn't snow much more that night, they would be able to keep warm enough beneath the shelter the trees offered.

"Lay down on that blanket, Jade, close to the fire," he instructed. Aston was used to the cold; he was worried about the princess. No doubt she'd spent every winter's night in front of a fire with a steaming cup of hot tea in her hands. Being out in the extremes like this would be hard on her.

Once Jade had lain down, Aston covered her with the wool blanket he'd given her as well as the blanket from her pack. When he was sure he'd made her as comfortable as he could, he disappeared into the woods to find food.

Jade lay there, shivering, wishing Aston would come back. She didn't like being out here by herself. It reminded her too much of the night outside Fridel when the wolves had been chasing her. She cowered under the blankets Aston had given her and scooted closer to the fire, hoping the flames would protect her until Aston returned.

She didn't have to worry for long. Aston returned within the hour, carrying three dead hares. She used to cringe at the sight of them, but she was getting comfortable with Aston's hunting. Now, she found it intriguing, watching the way he treated the dead animals as if they were still alive, still precious. He skinned them with such care, emptied them out like they were simply ill and he was helping them. When he placed them over the fire and washed his hands using water from his leather canteen, he came to her.

Jade didn't have to ask to know what Aston wanted. She moved away from the fire, allowing him room to lie down. Once he was beside her, she unraveled herself from one of the blankets and tossed it over him. Seemingly unsatisfied, Aston took the blanket that was still wrapped around her and pulled it free, tucking himself in beside her before encompassing them both in the blankets.

Jade was surprised at how warm Aston's skin was. With how long he'd been out in the cold, she'd been sure his skin would feel like ice against hers. Instead, he was like a warm hearth. His heated arms wrapped around her chilled flesh, causing goose bumps that were in no way related to the cold. Inside the cocoon of his arms, she almost forgot that she'd been nearly frozen only moments before.

"No use wasting body heat," Aston said, jerking her from her thoughts.

"You don't have to have a reason to hold me, Aston," Jade replied, tucking her head underneath his chin. She buried her face in his shirt, noticing for the first time how he smelled. The knight smelled like pine trees and sweat. While it wasn't a combination she would normally have thought of as appealing, for Aston it just fit.

"I wasn't trying to give it reason. I was just stating a fact," Aston told her, resting his chin on top of her head. Smiling, Jade leaned up and stole a kiss, loving the fact that she could make the knight defensive.

He returned her kiss wholeheartedly, moving his tongue along her bottom lip. Jade smiled into the kiss, and he took the opportunity to slide his tongue into her mouth, running it along her teeth before withdrawing again. He felt more than heard Jade's disappointed moan when he broke the kiss.

Aston uncovered himself and slid from the blankets, settling them back over Jade. He looked over his shoulder at her once he reached the fire, smiling when he caught her watching him.

"What will you do, Aston? When you're a free man again, where will you go?" she asked him, turning on her side, placing her elbow on the ground, and resting her head on her fist.

"I'm not sure. I don't think I want to go back to Fridel. I love being a knight, but this journey has made me question so many things I thought I knew," Aston replied, staring at Jade. The firelight was playing over her body, making her auburn hair dance with color. She looked beautiful.

"Where will you go, then? If I asked you to come to Adion, fight for my father, would you?"

Aston looked away then. He meant what he said; he loved being a knight, and he respected King Aric more than many of the other monarchs he'd met. Aric was the one king Aston always felt saw his soldiers as more than lives to throw away. However, he didn't think he wanted to fight for him. He didn't know if he wanted to fight for anyone anymore, other than himself.

"I like this freedom, Jade. I love feeling like I can go anywhere I want, *do* anything I want. I don't know if I want to go back to being someone's soldier," he answered honestly.

Jade nodded in understanding.

"For now, I'm happy doing this. Travelling…with you," he said.

Jade looked up at him and smiled. "I like this, too. It's better than being a prize on Jacob's arm," she replied.

"What will you do when you go back to Adion? Your father will make you marry the marquess."

"I don't intend to go back." Jade narrowed her eyes at Aston as his eyes widened. "What? You're allowed to run away forever, but I'm not?" she asked him.

"I didn't think you would want to leave your father forever. King Aric is a kind man," Aston replied, turning his attention back to their dinner.

"My father *is* kind, but he doesn't understand me. I can't spend my life as a trophy. I want to *be* somebody, really *matter* to the world. I can't do that as Marchioness of Summerslade," she told him.

Aston nodded. "You're welcome to stay with me until you figure out where you want to go," he offered.

"Thank you, Aston. I really appreciate it," Jade replied, sitting up and moving closer to him. She wrapped one of the two blankets covering her around his shoulders, shielding him at least partially from the cold. She wrapped her own blanket tighter around herself as Aston pulled the rabbits from the flames and began cutting them up.

After eating, Aston joined Jade under the blankets again, pulling her flush against his chest. She was so small; it was as if she were made to fit into his arms. Aston tucked her head under his chin again, loving the foreign feeling. In all his years as a knight, he'd never found a woman that touched his heart the way Jade did. She was kind, smart… beautiful. She was everything a man could hope for.

He knew he couldn't keep her. She was a princess, born with a duty to her country. He was no more than a soldier; right now he wasn't even that. He would have to find a way to send her back to Adion once winter was through. For now, he just wanted to spend as much time with her as he could.

"If we had no winter, the spring would not be as pleasant: if we did not sometimes taste adversity, prosperity would not be so welcome."

- Anne Bradstreet -

Seventeen

Jade was getting used to waking at dawn. She was even becoming better at tacking her horse. In the short amount of time she'd spent with Aston, she'd learned so much about herself and the world beyond the palace. She'd learned that someone could grow close to your heart in a single month. She'd found that the food you eat doesn't just appear when you ring a bell; someone has to prepare it. Also, she'd learned that sunrise and sunset were the most beautiful times of the day, times that she'd always missed when she'd lived at the palace.

If so much could change in such a short amount of time, what would an entire winter with Aston do to her?

She finished packing her satchel and attached it to Edward's saddle. Aston was covering their fire, hiding their tracks; Sterling was already tacked and ready to go.

"Will we make it to Delgrab's before nightfall?" she asked, finishing with Edward and tucking her hands into the sleeves of her blouse. Winter was just beginning, but already the air was too cold for her liking. She dreaded the day ahead, but if she knew she would have a warm fire and four walls around her by nightfall, she knew she could manage.

"We should, as long as nothing holds us up," the knight replied, looking over his shoulder at her before swinging into the saddle with practiced ease. Jade followed suit, mounting Edward, before the two exited the forest and returned to the main road. She found herself taking everything in; the trees were all gold, red, and brown. The thin patches of grass visible beneath the snow were withering away.

"It's so beautiful," she said aloud, more to herself than as actual conversation.

"It is, isn't it?" Aston replied. He looked behind himself at Jade, slowing Sterling down so he could ride beside her. "Don't you ever venture outside your palace?" he asked, raising a brow in surprise.

She shook her head. "I used to ride Bella in the spring and summer, but winter was always such a busy time. We had King Roland's ball and all of the servants took time away to see their families. I spent my winters inside, reading books in the library or helping Matilda sew in between lessons," she answered.

"Who's Matilda? And you sew?" Aston asked, raising an eyebrow at her.

Jade laughed. "She's my maid. Well, she was. She said her mother taught her to sew, and when I was young, she helped me to learn. She made the majority of the dresses in my closet," she replied, smiling. "I wish things were different. I wish my father would let me marry who I wanted so I could go home."

"That would be best," Aston said, not meeting her eyes.

Jade turned to the knight, but he kept his eyes trained on the road ahead, his mouth a firm line. Had she hurt his feelings, talking about home? "When we clear your name, you can go home too, Aston," she said, hoping to make him feel better. If anything, it seemed to make him more distant.

"Of course, Jade," he stilted. They rode in silence for a while, Jade wondering what her knight was thinking about and wishing he would share a little bit more of himself in the time they had left together.

**

Richie entered Delgrab's clearing shortly before dark. He jumped from his horse and raced to the door, pounding on the hard wood surface. Delgrab answered it, looking over the boy's head in confusion before looking down.

"Oy, Richie! What are you doing here, son?"

"I found a letter that I wanted to give to Aston. He said I couldn't go back to our clearing until he sent word for me. I thought maybe he would come here and you could give it to him." Richie pulled the letter from his pocket and held it up for Delgrab to see.

With a chuckle, Delgrab took the letter from Richie and put it in his back pocket, watching as the boy ran across the clearing and climbed back on his horse.

"Tell Aston I say hi! Oh, and Lady Jade, too!" Richie called over his shoulder as he left. Shaking his head, Delgrab went back inside. Aston had done a good thing, taking that kid under his wing. It seemed even Richie knew how lucky he was.

**

Jade sighed a breath of relief when Delgrab's cabin came into view. She pushed her heels into Edward's sides, coaxing the horse into a run. Aston did the same, making a race out of it. He let

Jade win, of course, but her laughter and smile were more than worth it.

Delgrab and Alys came out of the cabin as soon as the horses neared it, both sporting heavy bags.

Aston frowned. "Where are you two going?"

"Alys and I are going to spend the winter at her parent's home in Fridel," Delgrab answered.

"We thought you two might like somewhere private for the winter," Alys added.

Jade's eyes widened. "You want us to stay here?" she asked Alys. The motherly woman nodded, a smile gracing her features. Jade smiled and turned to Aston. "Can we?"

"You're sure it's okay?" he asked Delgrab. At his friend's pointed look, Aston laughed. "I was just making sure," he said.

"You two have fun. Oh! Before I forget, Richie gave me this letter for you." Delgrab reached in his pocket and pulled the letter out, handing it to the knight.

Aston jumped down from Sterling. He grabbed his friend in a firm hug. "Thank you, Del. You have no idea how much this means to me," he said, grateful he wasn't going to have to keep his princess out in the cold all winter.

"Thank you so much, Alys," Jade said, jumping down from Edward hugging the woman.

"We need to go if we plan to reach Fridel by nightfall, Alys," Delgrab announced, taking his wife's bag and heading into the forest. Alys gave Aston a quick hug before following her husband.

Jade looked at the cabin, her eyes shining. An entire winter with Aston in a cabin? She could handle this. She hoped.

Aston took Edward's reins from Jade and took their horses to the stable in the back, leaving her to wander into the house.

"The Rogue isn't going to go after Talbot until winter is over," Aston told her when he walked in.

Jade turned to look at him. "How do you know that?" Aston held up the letter. "What does it say?"

"King Roland's wife is still going to host their winter ball. She said her husband would be dishonored if she stopped the tradition."

Jade's eyes lit up. "Can we go?" she asked excitedly.

Aston only looked at her. "You are a runaway princess and I am a traitor. I don't think a winter ball full of royalty is the best place to go."

"King Roland makes everyone wear masks. It's like a …. a masquerade! It would be perfect for us!"

The knight shook his head. "I don't know, Jade. It doesn't sound like a good idea to me. Talbot, Donn, and your father will all be there. Surely someone would recognize us."

"Please, Aston! If someone recognizes us I'll protect you… somehow. I really want to go," she said, batting her eyes at him and pouting.

With a sigh, he relented. "Okay, we can go. We don't have anything to wear, though," he said.

Jade sat back for a moment before coming up with a solution. "I can sew! I'll go into Fridel tomorrow and buy material and buttons and I will make us costumes!" she exclaimed.

Laughing, Aston nodded at her. "Okay, okay, but I don't wear red," he said.

Jade nodded and smiled, excited. She couldn't wait to get her hands on some material! She had the perfect idea for their costumes.

**

Aston left Jade alone for a bit that night to hunt. She found firewood outside beside the cabin, stacked up against the wall. She brought a fair amount inside and started a fire in the hearth, placing more in the wood box under the make-shift stove. When Aston returned, she helped him cook for the first time.

Alys's kitchen was filled with fruits and vegetables, things she and Delgrab had picked and then left for Jade and Aston to use. Jade put carrots, potatoes, and rabbit meat into a large metal pot and set it to simmer, making stew for the night. Then she and Aston moved to the couch while dinner cooked.

"Tell me more about yourself, Aston."

Aston looked over at her and shrugged. "There's not much to tell."

"Come on, Aston. You didn't come into the world the way you are now. You had to grow up somewhere."

"I grew up in Fridel. My father and baby sister still live there. I can't imagine what they must think of me, knowing I'm a traitor," the knight answered, turning away.

Jade placed a reassuring hand on his shoulder. "You aren't a traitor, Aston. I plan on proving that."

He nodded at her before continuing. "I used to spend my summers out here, with Delgrab. His father owned this cabin before Delgrab did. He decided to move the family into town one winter but Delgrab wanted to stay here. He and I spent every day out in this forest, playing around and making up games like kids do." Aston smiled as he remembered. "I always told Delgrab that I would be a real knight one day, but he never believed me."

"But you made it," Jade said, loving his story. Her Aston had been a kid once, playful, with dreams. Now he was a proud man with a ruined reputation.

"Even if you do prove to King Donn that I'm innocent, I won't be a knight anymore," Aston told her, as if reading her thoughts. His face turned somber as he continued. "It will be hard to convince everyone in Fridel that their prince is a coward. No one will want to believe it."

"I wouldn't say Talbot is a coward," Jade replied, taking his hand. "He was just more worried about ruining his own reputation than he was about yours."

"That sounds like a coward to me," he told her, shifting slightly in his seat. He was too comfortable sitting there with Jade's hand in his. He had to remember this was ending soon.

Clearing his throat, Aston stood and went to the kitchen to check on dinner. An entire winter locked away in a cabin with his princess? What mess had he gotten himself into? *Already* her nearness was affecting him. He needed to distance himself from her, but that would be impossible in this small home. Aston knew he was falling for Jade, but he didn't want to. He wanted to send her home to Adion, make her marry Duke Aeron's son and go back to the life he had before.

At the same time, he wanted to hold on to Jade and kill any man who looked at her with lust in his eyes. He wanted to make Jacob of Northsbury run home and never return.

What am I going to do? he asked himself, looking over his shoulder at Jade. She was sitting on the couch, her favorite book in her lap. She glanced up and smiled at him, but Aston quickly turned away.

It was going to be a long winter.

**

Talbot paced his room, glancing out his window every time he passed it. He half expected to see The Rogue Royal riding up at any moment; he knew his thought was ridiculous. He didn't know what the Rogue looked like, and the murderer *certainly* didn't go to the murder site in the middle of the day.

Still, he couldn't be immobile.

The prince left his chambers and went to the throne room, hoping his father would be there. Luckily, he was. Talbot walked hesitantly up the red carpet, stopping in front of King Donn.

"Any news, Father?"

Donn looked up from the scroll he was reading, looking back down when he saw that it was Talbot bothering him. "What are you talking about, Talbot?" he asked, his voice a low drawl.

Talbot flinched; his father was still angry. "Have you received word of The Rogue Royal?" the prince elaborated.

Donn dropped the scroll into his lap and folded his hands over it. "The Rogue Royal is not killing anyone until after the winter season," he announced.

Talbot relaxed at his father's words. He felt every bit of tension leave him. He bowed to his father and turned to leave.

"Oh, Talbot," King Donn added. He turned to his father. "King Roland's ball has not been cancelled. I expect you to be well mannered once we arrive. Pity, poor Queen Eve has to see you there when you allowed her husband to die," Donn said. He then waved Talbot off, dismissing him with a slight flick of his wrist.

"Imagine how disappointed he would be if he knew you let Duke Aeron die, too," he whispered to himself as he went back to his room. He had the entire winter to think of a plan to save his life. He swore to himself, and to the Powers above, that, if he lived, he would right every wrong he'd ever created in his life.

"People don't notice whether its winter or summer when they're happy."
- Anton Chekhov -

Eighteen

Jade went to town alone the next morning. Aston didn't want to risk someone recognizing him and Jade didn't blame him. She wrapped herself in a cloak she found in Alys's closet and took Edward into town.

She had never been to Fridel. The princess found herself taking everything in, loving the smells of bread baking and the sounds of children laughing. Even though it was early, the town was full of life. Every shop was open, though their doors were closed to keep out the winter chill. The last leaves were falling from surrounding trees; Edward's hooves made crunching noises against the street.

Jade stopped at the first dress shop she came to, tying Edward to the post outside before going into the small building. As she entered, she pulled the cloak's hood from her head, shaking her hair. The room was filled with material. It was a seamstress's dream. Red, blue, green and brown; the colors smiled down at her from the shelves, begging to be bought.

A plump, little woman came from a back room, smiling at Jade as she neared. "Good morning, dear. Can I help you with something?"

"I need material for a dress and a suit," Jade answered, browsing the shelves. She stopped at a green silk so smooth, it glistened in the dim light from the windows. "This one," she told the woman, who quickly came and took it off the shelf, bringing it to a small table at the front of the room.

Jade continued browsing. She needed something Aston would like. She found red silk and considered, a smile on her face, before moving on. She motioned for the woman to help her, hoping she would have a suggestion.

"I need outfits for a ball," Jade told the woman. "What should my prince wear?"

The woman looked at her selection for a moment before looking at Jade. "Why not match?" she asked.

Jade smiled. "That's a grand idea!" she exclaimed. She moved to the buttons next, grabbing silver for herself and gold for Aston. She also chose some white silk for accents on their costumes, as well as thread and several needles. "I'm also going to need two masks," she told the woman.

Smiling, the little woman went to her back room, disappearing from Jade's view. When she came back, she had two ornate masks in her hands. "Those are perfect!" Jade gushed, taking them from the woman.

"Anything else, child?"

"No, thank you. This is all," Jade answered, watching as the woman cut her material according to the measurements Jade gave her. When her material was cut and folded, Jade tucked the masks away inside the wrapped silk to protect them on the ride home. She gave the woman the money she asked for, as well as a little extra, before leaving with her purchases. She tucked the material and masks into the satchel she'd brought with her before climbing back on Edward and going further into town.

Several people eyed her as she rode past. Undoubtedly, they knew her to be a stranger. Shrugging, Jade continued. She recognized Richard following along after a tall, plump woman and she waved to him as well. He smiled his gap toothed smile and waved back before hurrying to catch up with the woman. Jade laughed as he left. Something about this town made her feel so at peace.

A bag full of seasonal fruits and vegetables later, Jade entered the forest, heading toward the cabin. She made sure no one was following her before she reached the clearing, not wanting to bring anyone home to Aston.

"How was your trip?" Aston asked her as she entered the clearing. His shirt was slung over his shoulder, his bare chest gleaming with sweat. He'd been chopping firewood, Jade guessed. Delgrab's axe was imbedded in a tree trunk, a pile of wood on the ground beside it. Jade tried to keep her gaze from Aston's exposed muscles, but she feared she failed when she saw his knowing smile.

"It was fine," she answered as her cheeks flared. She handed Edward's reins over to Aston and took her satchel inside. She heard Aston's laugh following her until she closed the door. Shaking her head, Jade went to the room she'd chosen for their winter stay. Aston was staying in Delgrab and Alys's room, but Jade didn't want to stay with him just yet. They'd slept on the same pallet in the woods, but sharing a bed was different, more intimate. She wasn't sure she was ready for that.

She carefully took the silk from her satchel, laying it out flat on her bed. She tucked the masks under the bed, not wanting Aston to see them before their costumes were ready. Having nothing else to do, she set to work cutting material, setting pieces aside as she finished them. When she had all of the pieces for her dress cut out, she started on the sewing. She didn't stop until she had both sleeves and most of the top done. That was when Aston called her, telling her lunch was ready.

Jade left the room slowly, wiping her brow with her forearm.

"Working hard?" Aston asked, laughing. She stuck her tongue out at him before grabbing a plate and filling it with the salad her knight had made. She went back to her room and grabbed her satchel, coming back to the kitchen to empty its contents onto the counter. Aston looked at her, one eyebrow raised. Jade shrugged.

"We needed more vegetables," she said. Aston shrugged as well and went to the table, Jade following him. They ate in silence, Jade thinking about her halfway done dress in the other room and Aston fearing what he was going to have to wear to the winter ball.

**

Jacob reached Northsbury late in the afternoon. He checked into Knight's Inn and walked the streets, looking for his bride-to-be. With her fiery red hair and pine green eyes, she should have been easy to spot. As it was, he was having no luck in finding her.

With a curse, Jacob realized he might be too late. If what the kid had said about Aston being innocent was true, then Aston would undoubtedly be trying to catch the one man who could prove it: The Rogue Royal.

The Rogue had already made his stop here and left again. Jacob was too late. He turned on his heel and went back to the inn, shutting himself in his room to think. He needed a clue, some way to keep up with Aston and Jade.

Looking out the window, Jacob tried to think of a plan. He didn't want to ride all the way back to Fridel. It would be a wasted trip if he couldn't find the servant boy from before. As his gaze wandered, his eyes landed on the castle.

"Of course… the winter ball. If I know Jade, she never misses it. Maybe she'll come," he thought aloud, sitting straighter in his chair.

One month; it was one month to the winter ball. He would stay in Northsbury until then, waiting for his princess to arrive. When she did, Jacob intended to take her back from Aston Smith.

**

"Are you really planning on going, Mother?" Talbot asked. He had been sitting in his room, alone, when the queen had come knocking on his door. Now, she sat on his bed with him.

"Your father thinks it best we make an appearance," she answered, looking away from her son.

"Can I stay here?" Talbot asked.

His mother shook her head. "We will all attend. Besides, you are safe. The Rogue isn't hunting until after the holidays. You may as well enjoy the winter. You don't even know if the Rogue is interested in you. You aren't a bad person, Talbot."

"I am, though, Mother. I'm a horrible person. I've ruined so many lives for my own gain," Talbot told her, standing and going to his window. He pushed aside the deep blue curtains, gazing out over what would one day be his kingdom.

∙∙

"That's the way of royalty, Talbot. No one ever made it to a position of power without stepping on some toes," his mother said, standing smoothing the wrinkles from her dress.

"That's not the point, Mother," Talbot sighed. His mother and father would never understand. They saw nothing wrong with the way they lived. To them, power was taken by pushing over others. Talbot didn't want that kind of power. He used to, but he had changed.

"You're going to be fine, darling. Now, go downstairs and be fitted for your costume. Your father and I have chosen to wear red this year," his mother said. When Talbot didn't answer, she sighed, leaving the room and shutting the door behind her.

The prince didn't move from his position at the window. Red? Red like blood. Why would his father choose to wear the color of blood? He knew how terrified Talbot was of the Rogue coming after him. Maybe that was *why* he'd chosen the color, to make fun of his son and his fear.

With a sigh, Talbot moved, leaving his room and walking slowly down the long corridor. It would do him no good, resisting his father. If anything, it would make the man angrier. Instead, he decided to go along with the king for now, but, if the Rogue *did* target him, his father would be sorry.

**

Aston had tried several times throughout the day to see what Jade was working on, but as soon as he opened the door, she would throw everything off the bed and out of sight. Now he was spending his time reading more of the book Jade toted around with her. He was almost halfway through it, finally reaching the romance.

Jade made fun of him for reading it, but what else was he supposed to do when she stayed holed up in her room all day and night? It had been almost a fortnight since she began working on their costumes and she barely spent any time with him. He'd been taking care of the horses, cooking, cleaning, and cutting firewood. The snow had finally made itself known, sticking to the ground and slowly deepening. The trees were completely bare, the temperature below freezing. Aston was worried they wouldn't be able to make it to Northsbury for the ball without freezing to death.

Jade didn't seem to be worried. She kept saying they would bundle up, pack their costumes in their satchels, and change when they reached their inn in Northsbury.

Aston startled as the door to Jade's room opened and she stepped out, closing the door behind her. He looked at her quizzically when she came over to him, perching on the couch beside him.

"You like my book?" she asked.

He shrugged. She didn't need to know how much he enjoyed it.

"I thought I could make dinner tonight," she said, changing the subject and standing. Aston watched her as she walked to the kitchen before going back to the book.

Half an hour later, the cabin smelled like roasted pheasant and potatoes. Curious, Aston set the book aside and went to the kitchen to investigate. Sure enough, Jade was pulling a medium sized bird from the brick oven, the bird circled with potatoes in the pan. He wandered over and reached for a piece, but Jade smacked his hand away.

"Where'd you get the bird?" Aston asked, shaking his hand to get rid of the momentary pain.

"Did you know there's a smokehouse behind the stables?" she asked. Aston laughed. He had forgotten about that. He and Delgrab had hung so many squirrels and rabbits in that smokehouse as kids that they'd been banned from it by Delgrab's father. He hadn't been behind the stables since.

"How did you manage to find the smokehouse when you haven't left that room in two weeks?" he asked Jade.

"You do sleep you know," she answered. Aston shrugged and left the room, hoping Jade wouldn't take too long finishing dinner. It smelled amazing and he was starved. He smiled when his princess came into the living area, carrying the pan with two cloths, and set the bird on the table. He joined her, cutting into the juicy meat and setting some out on the two plates already at the table.

It was love at first bite. "This is amazing, Jade! Where did a princess learn to cook so well?" he asked her.

Jade shrugged. "Matilda taught me more than sewing. She doesn't like to feel helpless, and she didn't want me to be just another pretty trophy on a man's arm. A woman is made to keep a house, not to look pretty," she answered.

Aston nodded and went back to eating, not wanting his food to get cold. There was a lot he still needed to learn about Jade du Halen.

**

That night after dinner, Jade joined Aston on the couch. He'd put the book away, hoping she would sit and talk with him for a while before going back to her room.

"Are you almost done with our costumes?" he asked her.

Jade nodded. "I have to put the finishing touches on yours and then I'm done. It's a fortnight until the ball, right?" she asked.

"Yes. We should leave in about a week, before the snow gets too deep for travel. We can stay at Knight's Inn until the ball."

"Okay. So..." Jade looked around herself, suddenly feeling awkward. Night had fallen, the moon hidden behind thick, dark clouds. The only light in the room came from the fire crackling in the hearth, and she found herself wishing it were brighter. She could barely see Aston's face, though he sat right across from her on the couch, his body turned toward hers. As the thought entered her mind, he leaned forward, carefully setting his lips against hers.

How long had it been since they'd kissed? A week? A month? However long it was, it was *too* long. This kiss was desperate, longing. It was a meeting of two sets of lips that had been aching for each other and were finally given what they wanted.

Jade leaned forward, pressing her lips more firmly against Aston's. He set his hands on her waist, pushing her back against the couch and settling himself on top of her. Remembering his shoulder wound, Jade put her hands on his chest and pushed back, breaking their kiss.

"Your shoulder," she whispered, fearing her voice wouldn't work.

"It's fine," Aston replied. He bent down and connected their mouths again, not letting her argue further. He needed to kiss her like a fire needed to breathe. He'd had so little time with her and he'd planned on seeing her every day of the winter. This was the end of their time together. Once spring arrived, he would go after the Rogue alone and send her home to be married.

Aston growled low in his throat at the thought of another man kissing her, touching her. He leaned back and looked down at the woman beneath him. Her eyes were as hungry as his, her lips pink and swollen from his kisses. His eyes asked her a question; her nod answered.

In one movement, Aston had Jade in his arms and was heading towards his room, never breaking their kiss. Once there, he set her on his bed and settled himself on top of her again, his arms wandering over her heated body. His hands found themselves tangled in auburn hair, sliding down slender arms and across a frantic heartbeat. He pulled her dress down to expose her collar bone, placing light kisses there as he pulled more.

Jade's mind was moving faster than her heart. She wanted to be with Aston, but she was terrified. She'd never been with a man before and Matilda had always told her that a woman's first time was painful. She was scared of the pain, but not of the man on top of her. His lips set her body on fire, his touch igniting something inside of her that she'd never felt before. As scared as she was, she knew that this was right.

So she quit thinking and gave herself over to the passion.

**

Jade lay content in Aston's arms. He'd fallen asleep moments before and now she lay listening to his smooth breathing. His breath tickled her ear, but she didn't move; she didn't want to wake him. Instead, she traced circles on his arm, her head resting in the crook of his elbow. Every inch of his front was pressed to her back and she suddenly felt whole.

She was in love with the knight. She was sure of that much. However, Aston's feelings for her were cloudy. Men would take any woman to their bed, and while she thought Aston might be different, she didn't know him that well. She could only hope, for now, that he felt the same way.

There was also the matter of Jacob to attend to. She wanted to go home someday, and she knew her father would be waiting there, Jacob's marriage proposal at his side. He would never understand her wanting to spend her life with a knight. Especially when her entire reasoning behind not marrying Jacob was so that she could rule one day. With Aston, there was no chance of that. Unless Aston wanted to be king…

No, Ernst would take over before a knight would ever be allowed to rule Adion.

Sighing, Jade tugged the blankets tighter around her, cuddling closer to Aston. The room was chilled, winter breathing in through the small cracks between logs on the cabin's sides. She should have been warm, beneath the covers and flush against Aston, but her thoughts made her cold.

Jade closed her eyes, hoping sleep would bring dreams and the morning would bring a solution.

"Action and reaction, ebb and flow, trial and error - this is the rhythm of living. Out of over confidence, fear; out of our fear, clearer vision, fresh hope. And out of hope, progress."
- Bruce Barton -

Nineteen

The next week passed quickly, comfortably. After their first night together, Jade became more relaxed around Aston. A little over a month with the man and already he was closer to her than her own brother, though the relationship was completely different. She was learning more about her knight as time passed, and she was beginning to think she would turn in her own brother just to see Aston walk free again.

The night before they left for Northsbury, Jade packed their costumes into her satchel, marveling at their beauty. She would have to thank Matilda for teaching her to sew. Without the skill, she knew Aston would never have gone to the winter ball with her.

As it was, Aston was still nervous. Every time she mentioned the ball, his shoulders would tense and his expression would turn harsh. Jade knew he was scared someone would recognize him, but their costumes were perfect. She was confident no one would know either of them.

Her satchel packed, Jade left her room and went to Aston's. Ever since the night when she'd given herself to him completely she'd been sharing his bed. Her knight was already there, nestled under the covers. His even breathing told her he was asleep, and she carefully slid into bed beside him, hoping not to wake him.

A week from tonight, we will be at the winter ball, dancing together for the first time! Jade thought, smiling in anticipation. She closed her eyes and drifted to sleep, dreading the coming ride but excited about what would come after.

**

Aston awoke early the next morning, sliding out of bed before Jade had woken. He made his way to the kitchen, rubbing the sleep from his eyes and running a hand through his disheveled hair. He rummaged through the cupboard, trying to find something to make breakfast. They would need their strength for the ride, not to mention a full belly was often warmer than an empty one.

After a quick trip to the smokehouse, Aston had bacon sizzling on top of a fire and was in the midst of mixing ingredients into batter when Jade walked in the room. She sat heavily at the table, resting her head on her folded arms.

"Still tired?" he asked her, chuckling under his breath.

Jade didn't answer. Instead, she lifted her head from her arms, stared him down, and then went right back to resting on the table. Aston laughed aloud before taking the bacon from the metal skillet and replacing it with a little bit of the batter he'd created.

The princess lifted her head again as breakfast smells assaulted her senses. "Are you making hotcakes?" she asked, standing and moving to look over Aston's shoulder.

He nodded and turned, shocked by how close she was. If he leaned forward just a little, he could kiss her. With a mental shrug, he did just that, pressing his lips to hers before pulling away and returning to his cooking.

As soon as the small, round, sweet-battered disks were done, Aston filled two plates and carried them to the table. He set one in front of Jade and kept the other for himself. He handed her a jar of homemade honey that he'd found in the cupboard and watched as her eyes brightened.

"Honey? I haven't had honey in years. Father never buys it anymore. He says no one in Adion can make it right," she said, pouring a generous amount onto her hotcakes and taking a huge bite. Her eyes closed in ecstasy. "He should hire Alys," she commented before stuffing another large bite into her mouth.

Aston laughed, covering his own plate in the sticky, sweet gel.

When breakfast was over, he grabbed their satchels and went outside. He crunched through the snow to the stables, shaking stray flakes from his hair. Sterling and Edward looked at him warily; he understood. If he was a horse, he wouldn't want to walk around in the snow either, especially not for two days.

As he saddled his horse, Jade walked in and went to Edward. He could hear her whispering to the horse as she got him ready to go. The knight smiled and shook his head.

It didn't take long for them to reach the road to Northsbury. The snow on the dirt path wasn't too deep. Deep ruts cut through the snow, left behind by royal chariots. This was the most common road to their destination and other monarchs had undoubtedly already made the long trek, relaxing in the palace before the big night. It was through these ruts that they rode.

Jade had Aston's cloak wrapped around her again, her hands buried deep inside it. She didn't know how he made it through the winter, how he went along as if the cold didn't affect him. Now, trekking through the snow, all he had on was a long sleeved white tunic, brown pants, and brown boots. Jade was bundled up in her pants and blouse and her black riding boots, as well as the cloak, and she was *still* cold.

Jade shivered, looking at Aston, wishing she were as warm as he seemed to be.

It was going to be a *long* two days.

**

Talbot paced the room, his soft boots padding gently against the elegant rug. The carriage he'd shared with his mother and father had arrived at Northsbury early that morning, and now all he had to do was wait.

His father had barely spoken to him since King Roland had been killed. He was still upset with Talbot, still saying the prince should have done something other than wait in the bushes. When had he become little more than another soldier to his father? When had his life become less important? Talbot stopped pacing; he knew the answer to that question.

"When Aston Smith disappointed him," he thought aloud. He shook his head and clasped his arms behind his back, resuming his pacing. Aston had been his father's finest soldier, and Talbot had been the one to bear the news of Aston's betrayal. He'd lost all standing with his father that day.

Tired of his incessant pacing, the prince sat on the bed, sinking into the soft mattress. He laid back with a defeated plop and stared at the ceiling, crossing his arms under his head.

"Aston Smith. Who knew that by condemning you, I would also condemn myself?"

**

Jacob arrived at the palace of Queen Eve and the former King Roland a bit before noon. With the ball a week away, he'd decided to move to the palace from the inn and stay with the other royalty arriving early. Queen Eve sat beside him in the library, an old volume open in her lap. The marquess glanced at her, noting the bags under her eyes, the way her hair fell limply around her shoulders. Grief had not been kind to the lady. Even her blue eyes seemed dimmer than usual.

"Your majesty," he started, but stopped, unsure of what to say. He couldn't count how many summers he had spent in this palace, studying with his father. Now, both his father and the kind King Roland were dead. It amazed him how fast everything changed.

"No need for formalities, Jacob. You know I think of you as my own son," Eve scolded, turning her eyes to him.

Jacob nodded and looked away. "I'm sorry, Eve. I wish I could have been here," he offered.

The queen smiled at him, though the expression was forced. "There's nothing you could have done, Jacob. Lady Jade was here with her father's finest knight, and even *he* ended up injured."

Jacob whipped his head to the side to meet Eve's eyes. "Jade was here? With Sir Aston Smith?"

The woman shook her head. "I know not what his name was. I know only that he arrived with Lady Jade about an hour before my husband was murdered. Jade was with him, in the room with The Rogue Royal. I don't know how she managed to escape, but a servant of mine saw her rush from the room before my husband screamed."

"I'm so sorry. I'm sure the princess was terrified, being in the same room as that monster. She must have seen his face," Jacob said, leaning closer to the frail woman and setting his hand lightly atop her knee.

Again, the queen shook her head at him. "He wore a mask, my servant said. No one recognized him."

"Have you heard from Lady Jade? Is she attending the winter ball next week?"

"I received word from King Aric that he has not heard from his daughter in a month or more. He was unaware she had been here. Your guess is as good as anyone's," Eve replied. She stood then, filing her book back onto one of the library's many shelves. "Be comfortable, Jacob. There is a week until the ball and more royalty is arriving daily. Don't fret about what cannot be changed." The queen set her hand gently on Jacob's shoulder before leaving the marquess alone with his thoughts.

**

Ernst was uncomfortable. Seated across from his mother and father in their carriage, he felt like a stranger. No one spoke; what was there to say when you rarely saw each other? He looked out his window, watching the brown and white countryside ease past. It was customary for him to attend the winter ball with his family, but it was odd without Jade seated beside him.

Jade had known who he was from the beginning. She'd been the one to find him that night seven months ago, covered in vomit and blood in his room. She'd fretted over him, searching for wounds before discovering the blood was not his. He'd cracked then, telling her everything; she hadn't looked at him the same since.

She used to be his little sister, the one he needed to protect. Now, she was the one protecting him. She'd had countless opportunities to turn him in, to tell everyone the Rogue's identity. She never did. Even now, traveling with that knight, she still wouldn't betray him. Jade was the strongest, smartest, *stupidest* woman he'd ever met. What did she have to gain, keeping his secret?

Ernst sighed and stared at the empty seat beside him. Would Jade appear at the winter ball with her knight? Would Aston Smith risk being seen when the knight was just as wanted as he was?

**

Jade breathed a sigh of relief as Knight's Inn came into view. After two days of riding and a night in the snow, she was ready for a real bed. She left her horse with Aston and entered the inn, immediately taking in a deep breath of the warm air. She rubbed her arms as she walked to the front desk, greeted by the same woman as before.

"A room for two?" Jade asked, looking the lady over. Her bosom spilled from the low cut neckline of her dress, leaving little to the imagination. Her hair needed to be washed and her makeup looked cheap, but there was still something beautiful about her.

"Fifth door on the right," the lady answered, handing Jade a small iron key. The princess paid and made her way up the stairs, stepping into the room she would share with Aston for the next week. She quickly unpacked their costumes, glad to see that the silk hadn't wrinkled much on the journey. She hung the costumes in the small wardrobe before lying on the bed, covering herself with the thick, wool blanket provided.

She was asleep in moments. Subconsciously, she felt Aston slide into bed beside her and squirmed closer to him and the heat he provided before sighing in content and falling deeper into her slumber.

**

The week leading up to the winter ball was uneventful. Jade still hadn't shown Aston their costumes and, as the night approached, the knight became more and more worried.

"If the mask doesn't cover my face, someone is bound to recognize me," he told Jade for the hundredth time.

"Stop worrying, Aston. The disguises are perfect."

"How many blond royals and nobles are there?"

Jade looked at Aston, a brow raised. "About a hundred," she answered.

The knight sighed and looked away, thinking he should have asked how many fiery red headed females there were.

Jade went to him, sitting beside him on the bed. "Don't worry. Everything is going to be fine. There will be so many people there, you probably won't see Talbot or Donn anyway," she assured him.

"I know, I know. I've never been somewhere I wasn't wanted before is all," Aston said, taking her hand in his and giving her a light kiss on the cheek. Jade smiled and stood, going to the wardrobe. She turned to face her knight, holding the handles behind her back.

"Ready to see your costume?" she asked, a smile growing on her face.

The glisten in her eyes scared the knight, but he decided to appease her anyway. "As ready as I am going to be," he answered.

Jade frowned at him but opened the door anyway, pulling Aston's costume from the wooden rod it hung on. She held it up for him to see.

The emerald silk was the same color as Jade's eyes. Golden buttons made their way down both sides of an emerald coat, finer than anything he'd seen before. Emerald leggings were partially hidden under a pair of brown pants that cut off mid-calf. The mask Jade was holding was half white with emerald beading lining the outer rim. The other half was green, elegant white scrollwork branching out from where his eye would peek out.

"That's astounding, Jade!" he exclaimed, standing and taking the garments from her. He peeked over her shoulder, hoping to see her dress, but she quickly closed the door and shooed him from the room to change.

"The ball starts in an hour. If you don't plan on making a grand entrance, I suggest you get ready now," she called after him, watching as he disappeared to the washroom at the end of the hall. She locked the door and went to the wardrobe, pulling out her own dress.

"This is it," she said, her nerves bunching in her stomach, before stepping out of her breeches and into the beautiful gown.

**

Aston shifted uncomfortably in the hall. He'd been finished changing for half an hour and Jade had locked him out of their room. Instead, he was stuck outside, smiling at people going and coming down the hall who looked at him as if he were crazy. Turning around, he knocked again.

"Jade, people are staring at me," he whispered, hoping she would answer.

"I'm almost done," she called back, and the knight heard her laugh.

Aston sighed and leaned against the door. If she didn't hurry, they were going to get their grand entrance after all. The last thing he needed was for everyone at the ball to turn to look at them when they entered.

As Jade stepped from the room, he feared they would anyway.

Her auburn hair was piled atop her head, some of her tight curls hanging down from their elegant perch. Silver stones adorned her hair, shining every time she moved. Her dress was the same color as his suit, the same color as her eyes. It fit tight to her waist and then billowed out, hiding every bit of her figure underneath its canopy. A bit of white tulle stuck out from the bottom, crinkling when she stepped. White silk lined the top and created a sash at her waist. The dress was tight across her chest, allowing just a bit of breast to peek over the top. She'd added small diamonds in her earlobes and her mask was made the reverse of his.

Aston stared as she stepped from the room. If he hadn't already thought her beautiful, his opinion would have instantly been changed.

"You look beautiful," he breathed, though he was sure the words weren't necessary. Surely someone as stunning as Jade already knew.

"And you look like a handsome prince," she replied, taking the hand he offered her. Now when people stared, he was sure they were looking at the woman on his arm and not at him. If he were those staring eyes, he would not be able to tear away from Jade either.

As they exited the inn, Aston directed his princess to the chariot he'd hired for them earlier in the week.

Jade's eyes lit up in surprise. "A chariot to take me to the ball? How noble of you, Aston Smith," she said, a smile in her voice as she allowed him to help her into the chariot. As soon as he was seated beside her, the coachman closed the door behind them and they were on their way to the ball.

"We should think of different names to call each other. I can't be Aston, and you can't be Jade. It can be a true masquerade," Aston gently warned, turning to look at the woman beside him.

"You're right. I hadn't thought of that," she answered, setting her hand against her chin in thought. "I always wanted to be named Bella." She turned her eyes to Aston.

"Bella it is. And you can call me Richard," he said.

Jade laughed and he smiled at her. "I miss that boy. I hope I get to see him again."

"Me too," the knight replied, somber. He'd gone a full week without thinking about his situation. Now it crashed down on him again. A light kiss on his cheek brought his attention back to the current moment.

"Everything is going to be fine," Jade told him again.

"It's the heart afraid of breaking that never learns to dance. It's the dream afraid of waking that never takes the chance. It's the one who won't be taken who cannot seem to give. And the soul afraid of dying that never learns to live."

- Bette Midler -

Twenty

Jade marveled at the palace as the coachman helped her from the carriage. Lit inside and out with candles and lanterns, the winter wonderland she'd come to know and love seemed more beautiful than usual. Sneaking a glance at the man beside her, she thought she knew why.

Aston looked nervous; his eyes kept darting around, watching for someone who might recognize him.

The princess took his hand, making him focus on her. "Relax. If you look like you don't belong, someone is bound to notice that you don't," she told him, giving him a small peck on the cheek. The knight took a deep breath and offered her a curt nod, kissing the hand he was holding before starting for the door.

Jade glided along beside him, looking every bit the lady that she was. She seemed to float along the ground, and Aston was suddenly insecure. Did he look like a prince, standing beside his princess? Or did he look like what he was, a man unworthy of holding her hand? Shaking the thought aside, he held his shoulders back and tried to appear comfortable, though he was nowhere near.

As they entered the palace, he was pleased to see that nobody turned to watch them. They were introduced as Lady Bella and Sir Richard before they were allowed to descend the grand marble staircase leading into the ballroom. Aston found himself staring; in all his time as a knight, he'd never stepped into a ballroom before. He'd never had reason to.

King Roland had spared no expense when this room had been designed. Fifty-foot ceilings, grand, marble columns, and rich golden tiles caught Aston's attention. A gold chandelier the size of thirty horses hung from the center of the ceiling, shimmering with candlelight and casting glistening lights across the room. A small marble slab rose from the ground at the front of the room, and that was where the violinists stood, playing slow, soothing music as pairs danced across the floor.

A tug on his arm told Aston that Jade was tired of his gawking and ready to head into the crowd. He allowed her to pull him forward, trying to look natural but feeling he wasn't doing a very good job. People stared at the couple as they passed, undoubtedly wondering why they'd never heard of Lady Bella and Sir Richard before.

"Relax," came Jade's urgent whisper, and Aston forced his shoulders to loosen and his frown to turn into a subdued and friendly smile. When he caught people staring, he nodded his head at them and marveled at how they would smile back and look away, as if his smile was the only reassurance they needed that he belonged.

As his princess led him further into the circling crowd of bodies, Aston realized one very important fact; he didn't know how to dance. Jade chose that moment to stop, turning to face him and taking one of his hands in hers while placing the other on his shoulder. He placed the hand she wasn't holding on her waist, but didn't move aside from that.

"I don't know how to dance," he whispered, eyeing the couples around him. They all moved the same, circling in the same direction, the men lifting their partners in unison. As a knight, there was no need for him to know how to dance.

"It's simple. Just follow me," Jade encouraged, moving her right foot toward his left. Aston moved his left foot back, then followed with his right foot as Jade moved her left. Soon, they were moving with the circle; right foot, left foot, right, left. "Now, pick me up," Jade commanded, and Aston lifted her into the air, watching as she joined the rest of the women in the room, her hands planted on his shoulders.

He smiled up at the princess, her eyes shining with laughter. He set her on the floor and the circle continued. Aston didn't stop until the song ended, and even then he didn't let go of Jade. Instead, he leaned down and kissed her.

"Thank you," he said when he pulled away.

Jade smiled at him. "You're welcome. Shall we get something to drink?"

Aston allowed his princess to pull him from the crowd, moving to stand beside her. Another song started, this one faster paced, and the knight was grateful she hadn't tried to teach him the new dance that began. The fast steps made him dizzy to watch, and he couldn't comprehend exactly what was happening.

A cup was pushed into his hand and Aston looked down. A small, metal goblet of yellow liquid filled his grip, and he looked at Jade with a frown. She laughed at him.

"You were off in your mind somewhere again. I had to bring you back," she explained, taking a sip from her own goblet. Aston brought the cup to his lips, puckering them at the overly sweet taste.

"What is it?" he asked, eyeing the beverage warily.

"Punch. It's a mix of pineapple juice, orange juice, and just a hint of rum," she explained, taking another sip.

Aston set his cup on the table. "Royals drink odd drinks. What happened to water or mulled wine?" he asked, looking around.

"It's almost Christmas, Aston. There's a reason it's called the season of high spirits," she laughed.

Aston laughed as well and stood behind her, wrapping his arms around her waist. He jumped when someone tapped him on his shoulder. Turning, he was met with stunning green eyes. The man wore white leggings with a royal blue tunic. A brown leather belt and brown boots completed the ensemble. The mask he wore covered only half of his face and was the same blue as his tunic. A silver sword cut across the mask, the hilt starting at his forehead and the blade slashing through his eye and down to his chin.

"You're not from these parts, are you?" the ebony haired man asked. Aston shook his head. While he didn't want to be recognized, he didn't particularly feel like lying about who he was either. "Where are you from?"

"Um.."

"Leave him alone, Ernst," Jade said from behind him.

Aston turned to face her. "You know him?"

Jade nodded.

"Well, dear sister, I didn't see you there," Ernst said, pulling his sister into a hug.

Jade pushed away from him, moving to stand beside Aston again, almost protectively.

Something passed through Ernst's eyes, but his smug smile stayed in place. "So, I've been found out. Ernst du Halen, at your service," he said, bowing low.

Aston nodded at him, bowing slightly; something about the prince made him wary. He had a fleeting thought that Ernst wasn't a man you turned your back on.

"It's very brave of you, sister, showing up here with your knight," Ernst said, glaring at his sister. She was being dumb; why would she bring Aston here? Did she want to get the man killed?

"Speak quieter, Ernst! What if someone hears you?" Jade scolded, her voice low. She glanced around, but no one paid attention to their exchange.

"What if someone were to *see* you?" he fired back.

"Do you want to dance, Jade?" Aston asked, stepping between them and taking her hand. With one last look at her brother, Jade nodded. As Aston stated to lead her away, she turned back around.

"Please, don't tell Father, Ernst. I'd just hate if something happened to Aston and I let our little secret slip," she said, giving him her most innocent smile.

As they once again disappeared into the crowd, Aston looked over his shoulder at Jade. "That's your brother?"

She nodded, not meeting his eyes.

"What did he want with you?"

"I'm not sure, exactly. I haven't seen him in a long time," she lied. She knew exactly why Ernst confronted her. As long as he kept his mouth shut, no one would recognize Aston. Unlike royalty, knights had no faces to go with their names in the minds of other royals.

"He seems…pleasant," Aston offered, unsure of how else to describe the man without insulting Jade.

"Oh, he is. He's a real *joy* to be around," she replied sarcastically, pulling Aston to a stop and resuming their earlier position. Aston smiled at her, and she knew she was forgiven. She prayed Ernst wouldn't tell her father she was here, or that she was with Aston. As much as she didn't want to turn her brother in, if he got her knight killed, she wouldn't hesitate.

**

Talbot had been leaning against the wall furthest from the dance floor for most of the night. Any brazen lady that came to him with the intent of asking for a dance took one look at his face and walked away. His black leggings were uncomfortable, his red tunic itched like mad, and he felt stupid wearing a mask when everyone could tell who he was. His steely grey eyes and dark curls weren't hidden in his disguise, and arriving with his mother and father had given him away.

He was Talbot, the unmarried Prince of Fridel, and he would *love* to dance with any lady that threw herself at him. Or not. He had too much on his mind to worry about dancing with princesses.

Sighing, Talbot let his eyes wander over the crowd, stopping as he noticed Ernst across the room talking to a couple he didn't recognize. Glancing closer, he realized he *did* know them. The princess' red hair was dead giveaway paired with the knight's dusty blond. Jade and Aston; so they *had* come. Talbot pushed off the wall, heading toward the trio. As he neared, Aston grabbed Jade and pulled her into the crowd, leaving an annoyed looking Ernst behind.

As he reached Ernst's side, Talbot stopped, unsure of what to say to the man.

Ernst turned to face him, his grimace immediately turning into a relaxed smile. "Talbot! I was wondering when I would run into you," he said, giving Fridel's prince a firm handshake.

Talbot copied his expression, grateful to find someone in the crowd he trusted. "I saw you from across the room and thought I'd wander over. Who were you talking to?"

"My sister and some man she dragged along with her," Ernst answered, looking away.

Talbot knew instantly that Ernst was hiding something. He also knew that the other prince knew of Aston. Surely he recognized the knight with his sister? "You didn't know the man?"

Ernst shook his head. "I didn't recognize him and he didn't tell me his name. I've long given up trying to keep my sister's suitors in order."

Talbot nodded. "I see. I think I'm going to retire to my room."

Ernst glanced sideways at Talbot. "I thought you enjoyed King Roland's winter ball."

180

"It's not the same without King Roland," Talbot replied before walking away.

**

Jacob ripped his golden mask from his face and threw it on the bed. Tonight had been his best chance at finding Jade, but there had been too many people, too many distractions. He pulled the gold shirt from his body, crumpled it in his hands, and threw it across the room before falling backwards onto his bed. The marquess folded his arms behind his head and stared at the deep red canopy above him. How was he going to find his princess? Where would she go next? Back to Fridel? To Adion?

He didn't love Jade, but marriage wasn't about love. Marriage was about ownership. It was having someone to clean the house, tend to the dishes, bear children and be obedient. Jacob couldn't see the Princess of Adion complying to the latter. His runaway princess was everything *but* obedient.

With a sigh, he stood and went into the private bath attached to his chambers. He grimaced at his reflection. His brunet hair was tousled and stuck out in various directions, and his chocolate eyes were underlined in purple from lack of sleep. There were indentations on his face where his mask had resided for most of the night. He'd been so busy worrying about Jade that he'd forgotten to take care of himself.

The marquess shrugged and stepped into the warm bath he'd requested. He sighed in contentment as the warm water soothed his aching muscles. He'd spent more time riding in the last two months than he had in his entire life. *Jade is worth it*, he told himself, pushing his body completely underwater. He ran the bar of soap provided over his skin and lathered his hair with it, the sweet, lavender scent more soothing than the warm water. Jacob automatically felt better being clean. He stayed in the water until it became cold; only then did he step out, dry himself with the plush towel Queen Eve had ordered for him, dress, and climb under the down comforter of his bed.

He planned to stay in Northsbury with Eve for a few days after the rest of her royal guests left. It had only been a month since King Roland had been murdered. He didn't feel right, leaving the queen alone with her memories. He would find Jade sooner or later.

**

Jade was exhausted by the time she and Aston fell into bed that night. The run in with her brother had worn her out, and she was thankful Aston hadn't asked her any more questions about the encounter. The knight was down the hall in the washroom, changing out of his costume, and Jade didn't bother locking the door as she stepped out of her dress. Aston had already seen her unclothed; what more was there to hide?

The door opened behind her and she turned, expecting Aston. She wasn't expecting Ernst to be standing behind her. She quickly grabbed a blanket from the bed and wrapped it around herself, hiding the face that she wore only hose under her dress. She strode toward her brother and locked the door behind him.

"What the hell are you doing here, Ernst?" she whispered, pushing him away from the door in the hopes that Aston wouldn't hear them talking if he returned.

"That's a question I'd like to ask you, sister. What were you *thinking*, bringing Aston Smith here? You do realize that if anyone recognized him he would be arrested and hanged, right? Or thrown in a dungeon to rot!" he responded.

"No one recognized him, Ernst."

"*I did,* Jade! And I'm sure Talbot did too."

Jade's eyes widened. "Talbot saw him?"

Ernst nodded. "He came to me after you two left and started asking questions."

"You didn't tell him--"

"Of course not, Jade! I wouldn't be here yelling at you if I wanted Aston to die! I'd be leading Talbot here!" Ernst said, his voice rising.

Jade cringed. "Please, keep your voice down. I don't want Aston to hear you."

Her brother walked away from her, running a hand through his hair. "What are you going to do, Jade? Run with Aston forever? Leave him, return home, and marry Jacob?"

"I don't know, Ernst! Right now everything is just… things are happening so fast! I found Aston in the woods outside Fridel and started traveling with him. I didn't know he was hunting you, Ernst. I don't know what to do. He won't feel free until he catches you, and I can't help him do that. At the same time, I want his freedom more than anything, because…" Jade cut off there, unable to continue. Her shoulders slumped in defeat.

Ernst sighed. "I don't know what to tell you, baby sister. There's no way for you to get everything. You can't have a happy, loving family *and* have Aston Smith. You have to choose what's most important to you."

"I know that, Ernst. I can't make Father happy and marry Jacob. I can't make *you* happy and leave Aston. I can't help Aston gain his freedom and keep you safe. When did my life become so complicated?" she asked, falling onto the bed and burying her face in her hands.

"When you fell in love with Aston Smith."

"We all need the waters of the Mercy River. Though they don't run deep, there's usually enough just enough, for the extravagance of our lives."

- Joan Agee -

Twenty One

The ride home was quiet and cold. Jade worried that Aston had heard her talking to Ernst, but he hadn't said anything when he'd come in that night. She had made her brother sneak out through the window so Aston wouldn't see him, and she'd curled up in bed before the knight returned to the room. Now, trudging through the snow, she felt the need to tell him her secret, but she couldn't bring herself to.

What if Aston went to her father and told him about Ernst? Her father's heart would be broken and her brother's life would end. Aston still wouldn't be free; he'd hang with Ernst.

The princess sighed and stared at the back of the man riding in front of her. He'd been quiet, undoubtedly thinking about where they would go next. In a couple of weeks, the snow would start melting and Ernst would go after Talbot. If Talbot died, there would be no one to clear Aston's name and his entire journey would have been for nothing.

As their cabin came into sight, she breathed a sigh of relief. Two days in the snow had been more than enough and now she wanted to grab her favorite book, start a fire, and not move until winter was gone. She stayed outside to take care of Edward, but then quickly went into the cabin, shoving out of her frozen coat and grabbing logs for the hearth.

Aston came in right behind her, following suit with shucking his coat and sitting on the couch. Jade sat next to him once the fire was started, leaning against his side. She breathed a sigh of relief when he put his arm around her. She'd been afraid he was mad at her for making him go to the ball, or because her brother had recognized both of them. He didn't seem to mind now, though.

"Jade, about what Ernst said," Aston began, and she tensed in his arms. "What does he know about me? *How* does he know about me?"

"Ernst knows a lot of things he shouldn't," the princess replied. Her brother knew every dirty secret there was to know within the powerful families of their five adjoining kingdoms. It was what had finally driven him to start killing powerful people off, one by one.

"That doesn't answer my question, Jade," Aston replied, looking down at her.

Jade sighed. "Ernst was just afraid that someone would recognize you and you would end up being killed," she told him.

"Why would your brother care if I died?"

"Because our father respects you as a knight and my brother is convinced you are innocent. He's kind of adamant about people getting what they deserve out of life, and he knows you don't deserve to die," Jade said, meeting Aston's gaze.

He smiled at her. "I suppose that runs in the family," he said, leaning down to kiss her. Jade sighed into the kiss, wishing she could tell him everything. Her life would be so much simpler if she wasn't hiding secrets from everyone.

"What are we doing until winter ends?" she asked, hoping to change the subject. She was tired of talking about her brother, and his name made guilt settle into her stomach. She wanted the feeling to go away.

"I have to go into Fridel tomorrow," Aston answered, and she whipped her head around to look at him again.

"Why would you go to Fridel?" she asked him, sitting up.

"I'll be careful, Jade, don't worry. The person I am going to see is an old friend. He'd never turn me in," Aston replied, pulling her back against him. Jade still wasn't comfortable with the idea, but she knew she couldn't stop the knight if he really wanted to go.

**

King Donn stared unblinking at the letter in his hand. He had known it was going to happen; with the way his kingdom was run, it was bound to. It wasn't, however, supposed to happen like this.

Say goodbye to your son.

Five words, but they meant so much. The Rogue was targeting Talbot. Donn glanced out the glass wall of the throne room. He could almost see the snow melting faster as he stared. As soon as the snow was gone, the Rogue would be here for Talbot; for his son.

Donn scoffed and strode across the room, tossing the parchment into the lit hearth. The flames quickly engulfed the thick paper, licking at its edges tentatively before devouring it. If he didn't know, then Talbot wouldn't know. If the letter didn't exist, maybe the Rogue would change his mind and attack someone else. Or maybe he would still come and kill his son.

Either way, the king wanted to feel no remorse, wanted no part in his son's death.

Talbot walked into the room. He saw his father next to the fire and joined him, staring into the flames. The king was glad the parchment was no more than crumbled ash. Maybe the prince wouldn't question him.

"Any news today, Father?"

Donn almost flinched but controlled his actions. He couldn't give anything away. "Nothing, son. No word at all."

"Thank you, Father."

He didn't miss the way his son relaxed at the words before smiling and leaving the room. The prince was a coward. If Talbot knew his life was in danger, he would flee and then what would happen? The Rogue would kill him..

No, Talbot would stay and meet his fate. The Rogue never struck the same family twice. Once his son was dead, he would be safe. His kingdom would never have to worry about the Rogue again, and he would carry on as usual. *It may seem cruel, throwing my son to the murderer, but Talbot brought this upon himself.*

That's what Donn told himself. If his son had been kinder, shown some respect, some love for his people, then he never would have been targeted. If Talbot had stopped the Rogue before he murdered Duke Aeron, his life would not be in danger now. So many things the prince could have done to save himself, but he kept failing. Over and over, Talbot allowed his life to slip further and further, allowed his future to become less certain and his fate to loom ever closer.

Why should the king bother trying to save his son's life when he was doing such a great job at ending it himself? Let the murderer come and take the failure off his hands. The kingdom would be better off without him.

**

Aston woke before Jade the next morning and slipped out of the room, carrying pants and a shirt with him. He dressed in the living area and made his way to the stable, deciding to take Edward instead of Sterling. Sterling was too easily recognized in Fridel, and recognition was something he needed to avoid.

The knight pulled on his cloak, brought the hood up over his head, and rode into town. The streets were nearly empty; everyone was inside where it was warm. The shop he wanted came into view over the top of a cobblestone hill, and Aston caught himself smiling at the familiar sight. Zane's Jewels.

After dismounting, he tied Edward outside and stepped into the shop, nodding at the guard stationed there while keeping his head down. Once inside, he lowered his hood. A tall, thin man came from the back, his face breaking out into a grin when he saw Aston standing there.

"Aston Smith! As I live and breathe!"

" Zane. It's been too long," the knight replied, grabbing the man in a firm hug.

The brunet man stepped back but kept his hands on Aston's arms, looking the knight over with his golden eyes. "It has! But why are you here? Everyone in Fridel is looking for you. I hear even soldiers from Adion and Azazel know of your supposed betrayal," he said, bringing Aston further into the shop and switching his sign around to "closed."

"It's true, Zane, but I can't hide forever."

"Well what brings you to my shop? What could you possibly need from here?"

"A gift. For a woman."

"Ah, I see. She must be very special, Aston." Zane led him to a case at the back of the small shop. Aston glanced around at the various tables and cases, but his friend didn't let him stop to look. "Trust me, Aston, what you want is back here."

Aston smiled as they passed a glass case filled with sparkling rubies. The walls of Zane's shops had all been painted to match the precious stones he sold. One was sapphire blue, another emerald, and another ruby. The back wall was white, and Aston knew Zane was leading him to his most precious collection of diamonds.

When Zane stopped, he pulled a small, square pillow from the case, setting it in front of Aston.

The knight shook his head at the diamond necklace laid before him. "She's from a well off family, Zane. I want to buy her something that no one in her family would think to get," Aston told him, glancing around the case. His gaze landed on a silver bracelet hidden in the corner. He pointed to it and Zane smiled, nodding his head.

"It's perfect," Zane said.

Aston agreed.

**

Talbot hadn't thought anything of the strange urge to go into town. He almost never ventured outside the palace unless his father forced him, but today was different. He'd woken up with the desire to walk the streets of the country that would one day be his, and he'd come across the one thing he needed to save his life: Aston Smith.

What was he doing at Zane's jewelry store? Curious, Talbot stood across the street, facing another shop. He could see Aston's reflection in the shop window as he left, pulling his cloak over his head again. The knight jumped onto a horse he had waiting outside and rode off down the street.

Talbot followed him, running to keep up with the horse's quick steps. As soon as they reached the trees, Aston sent the horse into a trot.

If it weren't for the light layer of snow still on the ground, the horse's tracks clearly preserved, the prince would have lost them. Instead, he reached the small cabin in the woods after Aston had already taken care of his horse and gone inside.

He looked the place over, rating it in his mind. It was nowhere near as grand as his own home, but the quaint little cabin seemed comfortable enough. Shaking his head, the prince turned his thoughts to the real reason he'd come.

He needed to get Aston to help him.

**

A knock at the door made Jade look up in surprise. She was sitting in a chair by the fire, her book in her lap. Aston was in the other room, changing out of his wet, snow-soaked clothes. Who could be at the door?

Setting her book aside, she crept to the door and peeked out through the glass crescent. When she saw Talbot, she pressed herself against the cabin wall beside the door. Another knock had her pressing her hand to her heart to stop its frantic beating.

"I saw you, Jade du Halen. Open the door. I need to speak with Aston," Talbot said.

. Aston chose that moment to enter the room and he stopped, staring at the door. "Is that…?" he asked.

The princess nodded, her face grim.

With a defeated sigh, Aston went to the door and wrenched it open.

Talbot was on the doorstep, his fist raised to pound on the door again. He dropped it when the door opened and stood there, staring at Aston. His face was unreadable. He looked nervous, scared, and determined all at once.

"What do you want, Talbot? By the time you make it back to the palace, we will be gone," Aston said.

Talbot shook his head. "I'm not here to turn you in. If I was, I wouldn't have knocked." The prince ran his hand through his dark curls, seemingly uncomfortable. " I just want to talk."

Aston hesitated before moving aside and allowing Fridel's prince to enter the cabin. He scanned the woods for signs of Donn's army, but he didn't see anyone. He sighed and closed the door, following Talbot to the living area where the prince waited.

"What do you want, Talbot?" he repeated.

The glanced around the room, looking at everything but the knight standing before him, waiting for an answer he wasn't ready to give. Now that he was here, he wasn't sure what to say to Aston. "I need your help," he finally managed.

The knight stared at him before laughing. "Why would I help you, Talbot? You're the reason I'm hiding in the middle of the woods, running from armies, and rumored to be a criminal."

"I can fix everything, Aston. I can make it right, but please, you have to help me!" Talbot exclaimed, desperation in his voice. At Aston's raised brow, he continued. "I think the Rogue is going to come after me."

"You're his next target," Aston deadpanned.

Talbot paled. "How do you know?"

"A brick through a window in Summerslade last month," Aston replied.

Jade shuddered and Aston knew she was remembering that night as well.

"Father didn't say anything when I asked this morning. When is he coming?"

"He sent another letter to all of the kings informing them he wouldn't be killing again until winter was over." Aston looked out the window. "The snow is almost gone now," he commented.

Talbot winced. "If you help me escape the Rogue, I will confess *everything* to my father about that night in Adion," he said, his eyes pleading.

Aston considered it for a moment. He'd wanted to help Talbot since he'd learned he was a target, but he hadn't expected the prince to come and *beg* for help. The prince had always been proud, though cowardly. He never asked for help from anyone. He only made orders.

"How did you even know the Rogue might target you?" he inquired, curious.

The prince shrugged. "I told Ernst du Halen about you, and he asked me if I was worried about becoming a target. I told him I wasn't and asked him why, and when he told me, I started to think about it. I've been a horrible person my entire life, but do I deserve to be murdered?"

Jade stiffened beside Aston, but the knight couldn't figure out why. Did she suddenly feel bad for the prince? Or was she worrying about something else?

"What do you want me to do?" Aston asked, intending to speak with Jade later about her reaction to Talbot's statement.

Talbot relaxed, his deep frown turning up into a small smile. "Plan with me, Aston. You're a knight; you can help me conspire against the Rogue and keep him away from me."

"You could stay here that night," Aston offered, but the prince shook his head.

"He would find me. I don't know how he does it, but the Rogue always knows the location of his target. It's like he's on the inside and knows every little detail about the lives of the people he kills."

"So, you want me to come to the palace?" Aston asked. When Talbot nodded, he stood. "I'm not going to fall for it, Talbot."

The prince looked confused. "Fall for what?"

"You come here asking for help, claiming you can free me, but you don't need my help. You've never cared about a soul in your life aside from your own, and this is just a clever way to get me to return to the palace and die for you," Aston said, clenching his fists at his sides.

Talbot stood as well. "That's not true, Aston! What you said about me, about not caring about anyone, it's true! That's why I need your help! I don't want to die, Aston! I need you to save my life, and if saving yours is the only way to make you do it, then I'm going to help you!" he exclaimed, striding forward.

Aston held up a hand up to stop the prince from coming any closer. Talbot stopped and stared at the knight, waiting for him to make his decision.

As far as Aston saw it, he had two options: he could help Talbot and have his help sneaking into the palace, or he could help Talbot without the prince knowing and try to find his own way in. He cursed under his breath, knowing what he had to choose.

"I'll do it."

**

Talbot left as night fell, hurrying so that his footprints wouldn't be lost in the newly-falling snow. He looked back at the small cabin with a smile on his face. With Aston helping him, he was sure he would live. If the Rogue showed up and he lived to tell about it, he would be sure his father lifted Aston's sentence and that the knight was able to walk a free man again.

"It is usually more important how a man meets his fate than what it is."
- Karl Wilhelm von Humboldt -

Twenty Two

The palace was quiet. Night had fallen and Richie found himself wandering the corridors alone. Most of the royal family was already asleep, though he'd seen the dim glow of a candle from under Prince Talbot's door.

He made his way through the palace, down winding staircases and passed closed doors. He wound up in front of the throne room. The massive oak doors had been left open. Richie looked both ways, searching for patrolling guards, before entering the room. He hurried down the red carpet, stopping at the foot of the thrones. The large golden throne looked odd without King Donn perched in it. He was such a fixture there.

Shaking his head, Richie grabbed what he'd come for, a folded piece of parchment addressed to King Donn. The letter stating when and where Prince Talbot would be murdered. With a small, albeit slightly sad, smile, Richie tucked the letter into his breeches and hurried back to his room. Winter was coming to a close. The snow was starting to melt, and the Rogue would soon be hunting again. Aston would want to know everything.

**

"Are you really going to go through with this?" Jade asked as Aston pulled his boots on over his trousers. He looked up at her but didn't answer. "It's suicide, Aston! You can't trust him!"

"I can't trust anybody right now, Jade. If I don't keep Talbot alive, everyone who knows the truth about that night will be gone."

"I'm still here. I can tell my father that Talbot came to me, not you. He'd listen--" She grabbed Aston's forearm, but he shook off her touch.

"No, he wouldn't. You've spent the last two months with a fugitive knight. Besides, you already told me your father doesn't care what you want. Why would he care what you have to say?"

Jade looked taken aback by the curtness in Aston's tone, and she let the subject drop. Richie had come by the night before with another letter, this one from the Rogue himself, stating the time and date for Talbot's murder. The snow was almost gone now, and the restless murderer seemed ready to kill again.

"I want you to stay here, Jade," Aston said, grabbing his coat and pulling it on. When she went to protest, he held a hand up to stop her. "I don't want you near the Rogue. Bringing you with me to Northsbury was a mistake. I can't protect you."

"You're a knight. Protecting people is what you do," she argued.

Aston shook his head, staring into Jade's eyes. "If the Rogue had decided to go after you in Northsbury, I wouldn't have been able to stop him. I don't want to feel that helpless again." He gave her a quick kiss, holding her face in his hands a moment more before walking out the door where Talbot waited for him.

"You okay?" the prince asked as Aston mounted Jade's horse. He nodded without looking at Talbot and the pair took off into the forest.

They arrived at the palace gate fifteen minutes later. The guard at the gate was knocked out. A questioning glance at Talbot told Aston that the prince seriously *was* going to keep him from being seen. They had approximately three hours before the Rogue made his appearance.

Talbot led him around to the back of the palace, jumping off his horse and grabbing a rope hanging from a window forty feet up.

"This is how we will get in," he told Aston, pulling on the rope to make sure it was still stable. The knight nodded at Talbot and the prince began his climb. Aston was surprised. The last time he'd watched the prince scale a wall, he'd taken his sweet time. Now, Talbot looked almost trained.

"The lazy prince is good for something... who knew?" Aston murmured. Talbot called down to him that he was clear and the knight grabbed the rope, starting his own climb. When he reached the window, he waited for the prince to tell him it was safe for him to enter before clambering in through the window.

"I told you I could get you in here without being seen," Talbot told him with a smile.

"No one will suspect our horses outside your window?" Aston questioned.

The prince frowned. "I'll be right back," he said, climbing back out the window. Aston laughed and watched as the prince reached the ground and climbed on his horse, heading toward the stables. Footsteps outside the door made him freeze and he quickly jumped under Talbot's bed. The door opened seconds later.

"Talbot?" King Donn called. When no one answered, the king stepped into the room and closed the door behind him. Aston heard the man moving slowly around the room. Donn's feet stopped next to the bed and the knight held his breath, praying he wouldn't stoop down to look. Thankfully, the king continued around the room, stopping at the window.

"Sneaking out through your window, Talbot? Some things never change," he chuckled. "Guess it won't be my fault when the Rogue slits your throat." Aston heard the king clomp back to door and then leave. He waited a moment longer before coming out from under the bed.

It wasn't long before Talbot returned. "Horses are taken care of," he said, his cheeks rosy with embarrassment. Aston only looked at him. "What?"

"Your father was here," the knight told him.

"Did he see you?" Talbot asked, glancing around the room as if his father were still there, hiding in the shadows.

Aston shook his head. "No, I was under your bed. He said it wouldn't be his fault when the Rogue slit your throat."

Talbot sighed and sat down on his bed. "Father has been difficult ever since you left. He knows it's my fault you're gone, but not on the level that he should. He only knows that I'm the one who gave him the bad news. He doesn't know I lied. Ever since, he's treated me like no more than a common soldier. Worse than that, even. I can't believe he didn't tell me that the Rogue was coming tonight."

Aston sat beside the prince. "What will happen to you when you tell him the truth?"

Talbot shrugged. The clock in the hall chimed once. He looked over at Aston. "Two hours left. I'll go get some food from the kitchen. Just hide again if anyone comes near."

Aston nodded and watched the prince leave, suddenly feeling bad for the man. Everything Talbot had ever done had been to please his father and now the king didn't care about Talbot at all. He hadn't sounded the least bit remorseful talking about his son dying. Could losing one knight really mean that much to the king? Aston didn't think so.

More footsteps in the hall stopped his thoughts and pushed him under the bed again. This time when the door opened, he wasn't sure who it was. They didn't say a word, only walked around the room. Aston heard a scraping sound and knew that whoever was there had found the grappling hook on the window and removed it. After one more circle of the room, the visitor left.

Talbot returned shortly after the mystery man left. He carried a tray of food: bread, cheese, goblets of water and a bowl of grapes. Aston ate quickly, not mentioning the visitor to the prince. A knock at the door startled them both. Aston grabbed one loaf of bread and a goblet and eased under the bed. Talbot let him settle for a moment before going to the door.

"Ernst! What are you still doing here?" he asked the raven-haired man.

Ernst smiled at him. "Your father invited me to stay, since the hour is so late. He worried about me travelling in the darkness when the Rogue is supposed to appear tonight," he told the prince.

"That's odd. My father normally doesn't care about anyone but himself," Talbot said, his brow furrowing.

The visiting prince shrugged. "I suppose he's trying to change before the Rogue decides he's next. It's almost midnight, Talbot. Best be saying your last words," he said before leaving the doorway and walking down the hall toward the guest quarters.

Taken aback, Talbot closed the door and wandered back to his bed, dropping heavily upon it. Aston climbed out and sat beside him again, tossing the last bite of bread into his mouth.

Talbot looked at him. "That was odd."

**

Midnight was minutes away. Aston was concealed under Talbot's bed, dagger in hand. The prince was in his bed, lying awake in the darkness. The Rogue Royal always killed his targets at midnight, right as the clock began to chime, echoing loudly throughout the palace. The door creaked open and Talbot stilled, hoping he looked like a sleeping victim and not the tense prince he actually was. No light came in through the opened door, and Talbot knew his killer had arrived.

Aston waited under the bed as the door clicked shut and soft steps made their way to the bedside. He always arrived too late to help the Rogue's victims, but not this time.

Talbot clenched the dagger in his hand tighter, hoping his sweaty palms didn't loosen his grip. He waited until the Rogue stopped next to the bed before springing up, grasping for the man beside him. He heard a pained grunt as his arm connected with someone's face, and then he was wrenched from the bed and thrown, face first, onto the floor.

Talbot groaned as he was grabbed by the hair and lifted, his grey eyes meeting shining green. His eyes widened.

"Er..Ernst?" he stammered. Ernst growled and spun Talbot around, pressing his dagger against the captive prince's neck. Talbot grasped at his arm, cursing himself for dropping his own weapon when he'd fallen from the bed. He came face to face with Aston.

"What are you doing here, knight?" Ernst growled. His nose hurt like hell where Talbot had smashed it and now there were two people who knew who he was. He'd been trying to save Aston's life, but now he would have to kill him, too.

Talbot cried out as the murderer wrenched his arm behind his back; Ernst was angrier at the prince than ever before. If Talbot wasn't such a selfish, spoiled man, Aston never would have been exiled and he would have let Talbot live. He pushed the cold metal of his ruby-hilted dagger further against Talbot's throat; the prince's whimper told him he'd broken the skin.

"Ernst, please," Talbot pleaded, his voice only a whisper. Speaking pressed the dagger tighter against his flesh, and Aston watched as a thin ribbon of blood slid to his collar.

"Please, don't kill him," Aston added, his hands in front of him in surrender. His dagger was held in his left hand, blade down. He didn't know if he could reach Ernst before he slit Talbot's throat. The best Aston could do right now was try to convince Ernst to let the prince live.

Ernst glared at the prince in his grasp before turning to Aston. "Why do you want to save him? You're the reason I *targeted* him. If he wasn't around, you never would have been exiled. You'd still be a knight and have your title. If I get rid of *him,*"- at the word, his grip on Talbot tightened -"your life will return to normal."

"If you kill him, I'll be *hunted* forever. Talbot is the only man who can clear my name," Aston said, trying to reason with Ernst.

"He *deserves* to die," Ernst argued.

"If you let him live, he's going to tell King Donn everything. My name will be cleared, and I'll be able to live whatever life I want. That's what you want, right? You want to kill Talbot so I can be free?"

Ernst returned his eyes to the quivering Talbot. "He deserves this, Aston. You aren't the only man he's wronged. Half this country will rejoice when their prince is dead."

"The other half will mourn," Aston argued. "He's becoming a better man. He's fixing what he's done wrong."

"Only to save his own life!"

"Does it matter? He knows what will happen if he doesn't change, and he's willing to make things right! Just let him go, Ernst."

"I have to kill you too, Aston," Ernst said, his eyes lingering on the prince before glancing up at the knight. "You know who I am. Talbot knows who I am. You both have to die."

"Jade knows too!" Aston shouted when Ernst's blade moved horizontally across Talbot's neck. The prince's eyes bulged as his throat was cut, but the wound wasn't fatal.

Ernst narrowed his eyes at Aston. "What *about* my sister?" he asked. The clock in the hall started its twelve chimes.

"Jade loves me, Ernst. She'll know you killed me. She knows I'm here. She's waiting for me to come home, right now. Are you going to kill her, too? She'll tell everyone who you are if I die," the knight said, rushing through his words as he heard the clock.

Ernst heard it too, but he hesitated. He cursed, knowing Aston was right. His sister was innocent in the ways of war, but she would never forgive him if he killed her knight. Furthermore, he could never hurt his sister. He would let Jade turn him in and hang before he'd hurt her.

Killing Aston would hurt her worse than any sword, any dagger, ever could.

Another curse found Talbot on the floor, his right arm bent at an odd angle, his left hand clutching his throat. He looked up at Ernst. "Thank you," he said.

Ernst glared at the prince and spat at his feet. "Don't thank me. Thank your knight. Thank my sister. Hell, you can even thank your father, but I didn't do this for you," he said. He sent one last look to Aston before leaving the room, slamming the door behind him.

The knight sat on the prince's bed, his knees weak. In all his years as a knight, he'd never been more scared than when he thought Talbot was going to die. A groan from the prince made him look at the prince, watching as he struggled to stand. Aston went to him, pulling him up and sitting him on the bed.

"You should go now, Aston. It's after midnight. Someone will come to see if I'm dead now that the Rogue has left," he said, sliding himself further onto the bed. Aston nodded and clapped the prince on his left shoulder before grabbing his grappling hook and tossing the rope out the window.

"Thank you, Aston. I'll make this right," Talbot said. The knight smiled at him before vaulting out of the window, sliding to the ground and racing into the night. Sterling was waiting for him at the main gate, just like he and Talbot had planned. He mounted and rode through the castle gates. Glancing back, he saw Talbot's room bright with candlelight. The prince was alive, the Rogue was gone, and Aston would be free again before the sun rose.

It was a beautiful night.

"To the outside world, we all grow old. But not to brothers and sisters. We know each other as we always were. We know each other's hearts."

- Clara Ortega -

Twenty Three

Aston stood outside for a moment when he returned to the cabin. Edward was still in the stable at the palace, but Talbot was supposed to bring him by the next day. The knight wiped his palms on his pants; though it was cold outside, confronting Jade about Ernst was making him nervous.

He'd been bluffing when he told Ernst about Jade knowing his secret, but Ernst's reaction told Aston that he'd guessed right. Jade had known her brother was The Rogue, but she'd never told him. She knew how important it was to him to find Ernst, but she'd just gone along with him as if she were ignorant. Maybe she was even in on it…

Aston shook his head at the thought. Jade would never condone something like that. She believed in life and redemption too much. But she still should have told him what she knew.

One more sigh and Aston opened the door, jumping in surprise when Jade rushed into his arms.

"I was so worried about you!" she exclaimed, wrapping her arms around his waist and burying her face in his chest. Some of

Aston's anger dissipated, but not all of it. He returned the hug for only a moment before pushing Jade to arm's length.

"We need to talk," he told her, and by the look in her eyes, he knew she understood. Jade nodded and backed away. She moved around the couch and sat down, patting the spot beside her, inviting him to sit. Aston did so hesitantly, folding his hands in his lap. He'd never been so uncomfortable around Jade. Even when they'd first met, he'd been more bothered by her than uncomfortable.

"I know what you want to say, and I'm sorry," Jade started, but Aston held a hand up to stop her.

"Why didn't you tell me? You've known all along that I wanted to catch the Rogue, and you always tried to stop me. I thought it was because you were afraid I would get hurt. Now, I know you were just trying to protect your brother."

"No, that's not it at all! I didn't want you to be hurt! I still don't! But I couldn't turn my brother in either. He's my family, Aston. If it were your father, or your sister, what would you do?" Jade said, wanting to reach out and grab Aston's hand, but knowing he wouldn't let her.

"I would do whatever I had to to protect them, but I wouldn't lie to the people I cared about to do it," he answered. Truthfully, he wasn't sure what he would do if the situation were reversed. If his father was a cold-hearted murderer, would he let the man roam free?

"I'm sorry about that, Aston. I really am! If you were anyone else, I wouldn't have hid it from you," Jade apologized.

"If I were anyone else? You lied to me because, what? Because you're in love with me? Because my life is over anyway?" Aston asked, incredulous.

"No! Because you're a knight! A soldier! I knew that if anyone could hunt my brother down and kill him, it would be you! I *do* love you, Aston Smith. I love you more than I have ever loved anyone or anything in my entire life! If I didn't, I wouldn't be here, in the middle of nowhere, fretting over whether or not I was ever going to see you again!" Jade said, taking Aston's hand in her own as tears formed in her eyes.

Aston looked at her hand, clasped perfectly around his own. He felt betrayed, but he understood Jade's reasoning. With a sigh, he stood, pulling his hand from Jade's grasp.

"We leave in the morning for Adion. You can take Alys and Delgrab's bed. I'll sleep in the other room for the night. I suggest you get some sleep. It'll be a long day tomorrow." Without another word, Aston left Jade sitting on the couch.

**

"Father, I must speak with you." Talbot knelt on the plush red carpet, placing himself at his father's feet. He hadn't sat on his throne since the day before Aston left; something about it intimidated him now. He didn't deserve to sit there anymore.

Donn looked down at his son, one eyebrow raised. "Go on, Talbot."

Talbot cringed at the informality, another thing that had changed in Aston's absence. "It's about Aston Smith." Where his father has only been halfway listening before, now his interest was piqued.

"What about Aston?"

"He was here last night, when the Rogue attacked."

"No wonder Duke Aeron died...Who would have guessed, a knight from *my* court!? Aston is The Rogue Royal..."

"No, Father! Aston isn't the Rogue! Aston saved me from him!" Talbot interrupted. His father had looked a bit too proud, imagining Aston as a murderer. Nothing he had ever done had made his father as proud as imaging Aston as the Rogue had.

"Oh...and you didn't apprehend him, Talbot!"

Leave it to his father to be a proud man one minute and angry at him the next. Talbot looked down at himself. His arm was in a sling and his neck was wrapped in a thick bandage. His father really wondered why he hadn't been able to stop Aston?

"I'm sorry," he said, instead of voicing his thoughts.

Donn sighed. "Is that all?"

Talbot had almost forgotten the real reason he'd come to see his father. "No, actually."

"Well, hurry up, Talbot. I have important things to do," the king said.

Talbot sighed. He knew his father had nothing to do; he was just tired of talking to Talbot and wanted the prince to disappear. "Aston is innocent. That night in Adion, I was the one who stayed behind while Aston went after the Rogue."

King Donn didn't say anything at first. He stared at Talbot as though he were a stranger, his eyes unblinking. "It was you?" he finally said. Talbot nodded. "You're the reason my best knight is gone." This time, it wasn't a question, but Talbot nodded anyway.

"I was afraid of what you would say to me if you knew that I went to make sure Lady du Halen was okay instead of chasing the Rouge. I made up the story about Aston so I wouldn't be the one you were disappointed in, but I didn't realize how far this would go. I knew Aston would lose his position, but I didn't know he'd be sentenced to die. I'm sorry, Father."

Donn stared at Talbot again, his mind whirling. Talbot squirmed at his feet, bowing his head again so he wouldn't have to look in his father's eyes.

"Where is Aston now?"

"What are you going to do, Father?"

"If you tell me where Aston is? Or if you don't?"

Talbot swallowed, the threat in his father's words making him shiver. "He's going with Princess Jade to Adion. We are to meet them there."

**

The ride to Adion was silent. Jade knew Aston hadn't completely forgiven her, but she'd hoped he would at least be civil. It was a day's ride to Adion, and the silence was starting to bother her. Talbot had brought Edward to them early that morning, claiming he had spoken with his father and that they would meet up in Adion. Aston had spoken to Talbot while Jade packed and then Talbot had left. Aston hadn't said a word to her since the night before.

Sighing, she brought Edward up beside Sterling and turned to Aston. His lip twitched, but otherwise he didn't move.

"Aston, I'm sorry! I know I shouldn't have kept secrets from you and I never will again, just please, speak to me!" she pleaded. Aston turned to look at her but didn't speak. "Ernst is my *brother*, Aston. I love him. I always will love him, no matter what he does, because I know that, deep down, he's still the brother I grew up with. He's still the boy that would pick me up when I fell and set me back on my feet. He's still the boy who always gave me flowers for my birthday and kissed my bruises when I hurt myself. He may not be on his path now, but I know he will find it again someday, and when he does, I want him to have the chance to fix what he's doing now."

"Jade..."

"He's no different than Talbot! How many people has Talbot hurt, and yet you still protect him? How many pointless wars has King Donn started? How many men have you killed to please your king? How is Ernst any different? The men he killed were all corrupt. The men you killed were just doing what they were ordered, just like you."

"Jade! I forgive you! I'm sorry. I understand what it means to care about your family. I know what it's like to care about someone so much that you would do anything to protect them, and I understand that you want to think your brother can change."

"He *will* change."

"Right. Let's just go to Adion, talk to your father, and pray that Talbot holds up his end of the deal."

"What happens if Talbot lied about telling King Donn the truth?" Jade asked, unsure of whether or not she actually wanted to hear the answer.

"If he didn't, then I am walking to my noose."

**

Adion came into view early the next morning. Aston hadn't made love to Jade the night before, claiming nerves. He'd held her through the night, though, and he hoped that had comforted her enough. He hoped she knew how he felt about her.

There was an uneasy feeling settling over him. His stomach was twisted into knots, his hands shaking on Sterling's reins. The grey stone palace looming before him only worsened his nerves and he prayed Talbot and Donn wouldn't be there yet. He wanted to talk to King Aric himself before Prince Talbot and his father arrived.

Jade reached her hand out across the space between their horses, settling it on top of one of his own. Aston clung to it tightly for a moment before letting it go, watching it drop back to Edward's reins.

"Home," Jade sighed, staring at the palace. Aston could tell she'd missed the beautiful palace, even if she had left willingly.

"We should find your father as soon as we arrive," Aston told her, and Jade nodded her agreement. They were let through the palace gates without a problem; Jade directed Aston toward the stables.

"Princess Jade! You're back!" Sebastian said, striding over to her.

"Yes, Sebastian, I'm sorry. I hope you didn't get into trouble."

"Not at all, Princess, not at all. King Aric is a kind man." Jade smiled at the old stable hand before taking Aston's hand and leading him toward the palace.

Aston took in everything around him. Fridel had been his home his entire life and he'd only been to Adion on missions. He'd never actually had time to notice the details around the grand palace. A rose garden passed on his right, full of tall trellises, climbing vines, and small fountains. Right now, the vines were brown, the winter having been harsh on the flowers. He could imagine how they would look in the spring, all the white, yellow, red and pink, mixing together into a symphony of colors and scents.

The idea striking him suddenly, Aston pulled Jade into the dying garden, into the labyrinth of crispy leaves and delicate thorns. She laughed as he led her through the maze, slapping stray vines out of her way.

"Where are we going?" she asked him. Aston finally stopped at a stone bench a little ways into the garden. Though everything was dead, he'd still managed to find a place where they couldn't be seen from the palace.

"I forgot to give you your Christmas gift," he said, guiding her to the bench. Jade sat down, folding her hands in her lap.

"When did you get me a gift?" she asked, her eyes widening.

"Do you remember when I went into town, right after we returned from Northsbury?" Jade nodded. "That's when," he answered. He reached into his satchel, which he had hanging on his shoulder, and pulled out a small, wooden box. On the top was a pair of hearts, twisting and spiraling and joining in the middle. Aston handed it to Jade.

"Aston! It's beautiful!" she exclaimed, turning the little box over in her hands.

Aston chuckled. "Well, thank you, but the real gift is inside," he told her.

"Oh." Looking down, Jade slowly lifted the lid. Her eyes widened when she saw the little silver bracelet sitting inside, her face breaking into a grin. The bracelet was nestled on a small square of black velvet. Hanging from the chain were two charms; one was a silver heart with a small ruby in the top, right corner. The other was a small, thin silver sword, emeralds set into the hilt. It was perfect.

"Aston... it's amazing," she said. Aston smiled at her and lifted the bracelet from the box, clasping it around her wrist. "How did you... I mean... it must have cost so much," she said, meeting his gaze.

"You don't need to worry about that, Jade."

"Thank you, Aston. I love it." Jade stood and wrapped her arms around Aston, smiling as she felt his arms close around her. He took her chin in his hand and lifted her face, giving her a light kiss.

"Now, no matter where you are, I will always be with you. I love you, Jade," Aston whispered. It was the first time he'd told her, but the time felt right. Though everything seemed to be fine and worked out, he couldn't help but feel that their biggest trials lay ahead.

"I love you, too," she replied. Jade released Aston from her arms and grabbed his hand, leading him back out of the maze. They needed to get to her father. They'd wasted enough time.

Past the garden, Aston could see the entrance to the palace. A cobblestone path, wide enough for a carriage, wove its way through the grounds and to the stairs before making a wide circle and then creating a path back out again. In the center of the circle was a large, marble fountain. The statue on the fountain was a beautiful woman, clad in only a shawl that wrapped around her ample frame before trailing off behind her and into the water. Water ran from a book she was holding, out over the pages and into the waiting trough below. Aston raised an eyebrow and turned to Jade, who shrugged.

"My family loves books. You should see our library," she said. Aston laughed at her, but he cut the sound short. Today was not a day for laughter. Today was the day his fate was decided. If he was still alive the next morning, he would laugh as much as his heart desired. For today, he promised to be subdued.

Jade practically pulled Aston up the stone steps. His feet weren't working right anymore. As they entered the palace, Aston found himself staring straight ahead, paying no attention to the various doors they passed or the paintings on the walls. A few turns later, he found himself looking into the throne room.

Tall white doors had been left open and Aston watched Jade walk through them and start down the green carpet. The color fit, as all members of the du Halen line were born with emerald eyes. It was a trait passed down from King Aric's grandfather and it had never been broken. Jade turned to stare at him and motioned for him to follow her, which he did, reluctantly. His feet sank into the soft carpet and the feeling relaxed him. His steps became less tense and more determined as he made his way down the carpet, staring at the man he had always considered a friend.

When he reached the foot of the thrones, Aston bowed. "Your Majesty," he said, lifting his head to look into King Aric's shining eyes.

"You received my message, Aston Smith. You've brought my daughter back to me," Aric said, standing and pulling Jade into a hug.

"I'm sorry, Father. I hope you understand why I left."

"Why you left, yes, but not why you have returned. Surely one knight couldn't drag my daughter back. Even Jacob, who has been looking for you for over a month, could not find you. He arrived back just yesterday! He will be overjoyed knowing you have returned!" Aric said, a laugh in his voice.

Jade frowned. "No, Father. Aston didn't have to drag me back. I came willingly. There is something we must discuss," Jade told him, leading her father back to his seat and settling him. She returned to her spot at Aston's side once her father was comfortable, ignoring his comment about Jacob. That was a conversation best saved for later, once Aston was free and she could tell her father who she *really* wanted to marry.

"Well then, dear child, do tell me. What is so important that you would come back when you wanted to leave so badly?"

"Aston Smith."

"I know who he is, daughter."

"That's why I came back. I need to talk to you about Aston, Father."

"I'm afraid I don't understand, daughter." The king furrowed his brow, his eyes wandering back and forth between Jade and Aston.

"What she means, your Majesty," Aston interrupted, "is that I never received an order to bring her back to you."

"I sent King Donn the letter almost two months ago. Surely he received it by now?"

"Yes, sire, he did, but he never told me those orders because I wasn't at the palace at the time."

"Oh, you had another mission then?" King Aric asked.

Jade answered him. "He didn't have a mission, Father. He was sentenced to death."

"Blasphemy. I see the man standing before me now," King Aric said, sticking his chin out.

If the situation hadn't been so dire, Jade might have laughed. "Prince Talbot told his father a story about Aston, about the night Duke Aeron was killed," she told him.

Aric frowned. "Tell me more, daughter."

"You saw Aston come back from chasing the Rogue, right Father?"

"Yes, yes. I set my hand on his shoulder as I passed him in the hall," Aric said, glancing at Aston. Aston nodded.

"Talbot told King Donn that *he* was the one who chased The Rogue Royal while Aston stayed behind," Jade told him.

"So, King Donn blamed me for the death of Duke Aeron and sentenced me to hang," Aston added.

King Aric nodded, his eyes narrowed. "I understand. Why are you here, then, Aston Smith?"

"Talbot and King Donn know I am here. The Rogue targeted Prince Talbot two nights ago, but Talbot came to me requesting a deal. He told me that if I saved his life, he would tell his father the truth about that night two months ago."

"And you agreed?" King Aric asked. Aston nodded. "Talbot and Donn will be coming here?" Aston nodded again. "And you want to be here when they arrive?"

"Yes, Sire."

Aric looked at his daughter. "Is this story true? Did Talbot really lie to King Donn about that night, get Aston sentenced, and then offer him a deal to regain his freedom?"

"Yes, Father. I was with Aston when Talbot came and made the deal," Jade answered.

"Very well. There is only one thing I can do until Talbot and Donn get here," he said. Jade looked at Aston, who glanced back at her before returning his eyes to the king.

"And what is that, your majesty?"

King Aric sighed. "Guards!" he called. "Arrest this man! Bring him to the dungeons!"

"When I saw you, I was afraid to meet you. When I met you, I was afraid to kiss you. When I kissed you, I was afraid to love you. Now that I love you, I'm afraid to lose you."
- Unknown Author –

Twenty Four

"Father, please!" Jade exclaimed, pushing Aston behind her. "Don't arrest him!"

King Aric looked at his daughter and sighed. "There's nothing I can do, Jade. King Donn has labeled the man behind you a traitor. I have to arrest him."

"But you *know* Talbot lied to King Donn, Father! You saw Aston coming down the hall after Talbot left my room! Surely you could talk to Donn and make some sort of deal," Jade said, her voice bordering on pleading.

"I'm sorry, princess. There's nothing I can do." King Aric looked at the ground. The guards chose that moment to rush in, grabbing Aston's arms and wrenching them behind him.

"No! Don't hurt him! Let him go!" Jade cried, rushing to her knight and throwing her arms around him. She buried her face in his chest, allowing her tears to seep into his shirt.

"It's okay, Jade," she heard Aston say. She looked up and her eyes met his. She could see fear in them, but his love for her shone brighter and she found herself believing him.

"You promise?" she asked, holding on to the childish idea that promises were always kept.

"I promise." Jade let go of Aston, then, and watched her father's guards take him away. Fear settled into her and she wished she'd kissed him before he disappeared.

**

His wrists were rubbed raw, his shoulders sore from the strain of being held above his head. Aston pulled at his restraints one last time before giving up. His wounded shoulder ached at its awkward angle, but he supposed it was fitting. Prisoners weren't meant to be comfortable.

How many men had he put in this same predicament? How many times had King Donn told him a man was guilty and then watched as Aston brought the man down?

How many of those men had been innocent, like him? Jade had been right about him and Ernst being the same.

Aston cursed under his breath. He was terrified. Ernst wouldn't come forward as The Rogue Royal and Aston couldn't reveal him without hurting Jade. If there was one thing he could never bring himself to do, it was hurt her.

The knight tilted his head back, his eyes travelling to a hole in the roof no bigger than a rabbit. The full moon above him allowed the dungeon some light, saving Aston from being immersed in darkness. It also allowed him a detailed view of his dungeon mate, a man who was no more than bones, chained across the room from him.

Is that to be my fate? To be left here, forgotten, until I completely disintegrate? He shivered at the image that passed through his mind. After all he'd been through, with all he'd found out, he still wasn't ready to die.

**

"I don't understand, Father. I don't understand why you think there is *nothing* you can do. You are the *only* one who can save him." Jade was seated on her throne, her father beside her. She wouldn't look at him. She had promised herself her eyes wouldn't return to her father until he set Aston free.

"What do you want me to do, Jade? Do you want me to release Aston Smith, let you run away with him, and tell King Donn he escaped?"

"No, Father. I want you to tell King Donn what you know about the night Duke Aeron was murdered. I want Aston to be able to live without being hunted. I want him to be given back his honor, and his title as a knight," the princess answered, setting her eyes on the throne room's doors when they threatened to turn to her father.

"So, you want me to tell Donn what I *think* to be the truth."

"You *know* it is! And so does Talbot! How many people did the prince address outside my room that night? They all know the truth as well! Even *I* know Talbot was with me when The Rogue managed to escape!"

"I'm sorry, dear. I can try, but I don't know how much good it will do your knight."

Now, Jade looked at her father, a smile forming on her face. "Thank you, Father! I am going to tell Aston!" She stood to leave, but her father grabbed her arm.

"Donn and Talbot will be here momentarily. Stay for now. If everything works out, *then* go and tell the knight. Don't give him hope when it might be wrenched away again."

Jade nodded and sat back down. She knew her father was right, but she wanted to see Aston. She wanted to kiss him and hold him. She wanted to assure him that everything would be fine.

**

Aston blinked as candlelight from the hall met his eyes, watching as a tall shadow came toward him. His eyes widened as he recognized the figure.

"What are you..." Aston started.

"Don't say anything," the person said.

Aston furrowed his brow in confusion; then, his eyes wandered from his visitor's face to their hands. One was clenched in a fist at their side. The other was holding a sword that was dripping blood onto the concrete floor. His sword. Aston struggled against his restraints, but still they held. He didn't want to die. He didn't want to leave Jade behind. In all of his years as a knight, Aston had never once begged for his life to be spared. Now, in the face of death, with his princess somewhere above him, he knew that was what he had to do.

"Jade--"

"Jade won't know. No one will. The guard outside the door is dead. By the time Jade gets down here, or anyone, for that matter, you will be too."

"Please...I swear... as soon as everything is settled, I will leave. You'll never see me again," Aston pleaded, setting his eyes on the sword. His visitor's sword hand twitched, but otherwise didn't move.

"I'm sorry, Aston Smith. You are a fine man, but I can't let you stand in Jade's way." They raised their blade, setting the tip against Aston's chest. He looked up to meet the eyes of his murderer, surprised to see a single tear slip from their right eye. "I really am sorry." As soon as the words left their mouth, Aston's killer slid the bloodied blade home.

**

King Donn and Prince Talbot arrived an hour after Aston was taken to the dungeon. Jade was still seated beside her father, her nerves making her squirm in her seat. Talbot's arm was in a sling, she noticed, but he smiled at her when they entered the room. Jade returned the smile, hoping Talbot hadn't gone back on his deal with Aston. If there was one person King Donn would listen to, it was his son. Without Talbot's help, she feared Aston would be dead by morning.

"King Donn, Prince Talbot, welcome," her father said, standing to welcome his guests. Talbot bowed slightly and Donn gathered King Aric into a brief hug. "Donn, I have a few things I would like to discuss with you," Aric began.

Donn held a hand up to stop him. "There is no need, old friend. Talbot explained everything to me yesterday morning. I'm sad to say I threw away my best knight without investigating the claims made by my son," Donn said, surprising both Jade and her father. Donn sent a sideways glance at Talbot, his eyes narrowed, and at Talbot's wince, Jade found herself wondering what Talbot had promised his father in return for Aston's freedom.

"What are you saying, Donn?" Aric questioned.

"I am saying you should free my knight," Donn answered.

Jade sprung from her throne and raced to Donn, throwing her arms around the man she had hated since meeting Aston. She then jumped on Talbot, careful of his arm, and kissed him on the cheek before rushing from the room. As soon as she was out the door, she ran into her brother.

"Jade! I was looking for you," Ernst said, catching her by her shoulders.

"Can it wait, Ernst? I'm going to free Aston," she replied, straining to look over his shoulder. The stairs leading to the dungeon were just to the left at the end of the hallway. She was so close, she could feel Aston's arms around her already.

"That's what I need to talk to you about, sister," Ernst answered, ducking his head to meet his sister's gaze.

She met his eyes then, her smile quickly disappearing. "What's there to talk about, Ernst? I said I would help free him and I did."

"He knows who I am, Jade!" Ernst said, keeping his voice low. "What if he turns me in? He's a threat to this family!"

"If Aston was going to tell somebody about you, he would have done so already. He knows I love you and he will never hurt me. Can I go now?" she asked, spinning out of her brother's grasp and continuing down the hallway. When she looked back, Ernst was walking away, shaking his head. She came to a sudden halt as she ran into someone else.

"Princess! I was looking for you," Jacob said.

Jade sighed and frowned. "So was everybody else, Jacob. Move, please. I have important matters to attend to," Jade said, exasperated. All she wanted was to hold her knight. What that really so much to ask?

"Jade, your father hasn't called off our marriage," Jacob said, successfully interrupting her thoughts.

"He knows how I feel about Aston. This marriage will never happen. You may as well accept that now."

"I'm not so sure," he replied with a smile.

"I really don't have time for this, Jacob," she said, moving around him. Jacob allowed her to leave, just as her brother had. She rushed down the stairs to the dungeons, taking them two at a time. She stopped when she reached the bottom. Beside the door, the guard was laid out on his back, his throat slit. Fearing what she would find, Jade entered the dungeon. She stepped as soon as she was through the door.

Then she screamed.

"When love is lost, do not bow your head in sadness; instead keep your head up high and gaze into heaven for that is where your broken heart has been sent to heal."
- Author Unknown -

Twenty-Five

Jade rushed to her fallen knight, quickly unshackling him and pulling his head into her lap. "Aston? Aston!" She screamed his name, praying he would open his eyes. She wouldn't even care if he called her princess, as long as he called her *something*! When those blue eyes she loved fluttered open, her breath caught in her throat and her heart jumped in her chest. He was alive.

"Jade?" His voice was harsh, choked.

She ran a hand through his hair, trying to soothe him. "I'm here," she answered, leaning down to place a kiss on his brow.

Aston sighed and coughed, placing a hand over the wound in his chest. "I love you, Jade," he said, fighting to keep his eyes open. He had to tell her one last time. She needed to know.

"I know you do, Aston. I know. Hold on, okay? Help is coming," she lied. Truthfully, she didn't know if anyone would come. Her father was still talking to Donn and Talbot. Her brother and Jacob were long gone. The guard outside the door was dead. There was no help.

"I love you," he said again, allowing his eyes to slip closed.

Jade wasn't allowing that. "No, Aston, don't sleep. I love you, do you hear me? I love you, Aston Smith. You're a free man again. King Donn released you. We can go anywhere we want to!" she said, shaking his shoulders gently. Aston smiled, but otherwise didn't respond. "Aston, *please*," she pleaded.

She had done everything she'd said she would. She'd traveled with this man, hated him, loved him, befriended him. He'd taught her to saddle a horse, to skin a rabbit, to make love. And now he was dying and teaching her heart how to shatter into a million tiny pieces.

As his heart stopped, she screamed, praying for someone to hear her, to *help* her. Her father appeared in the doorway, his eyes widening when he caught sight of his daughter kneeling in a pool of blood, a dying knight in her lap. Two guards came in behind him, the ones who had arrested Aston, and came to her side. She glared at them as they reached for Aston, daring them with her eyes to touch him. They looked to Aric for guidance.

"It's too late, Jade," the king said, coming to her side and grabbing her by the elbow. "He's gone, sweetheart. He's gone," he repeated, his voice soft.

Jade looked up into her father's eyes and saw the hurt buried deep within them. She looked down at her knight and found his midnight eyes partly open, frozen, staring at her. She let herself break. Her father pulled her to her feet and wrapped an arm around her shoulders, leading her from the room. No matter how hard she fought, he wouldn't let her return to her love's side. The last time she saw him, he was being lifted by the two guards, and not gently. She wanted to yell at them to be careful, but what was the point? Her knight was dead.

A strangled sob escaped her throat then as the gate holding back her tears broke, releasing the pent up agony she'd been too scared to unleash. She fell to her knees halfway up the stone stairs; had her father not been holding her, she would have tumbled down them. Jade pounded her fists against the cool stone, wishing she could join her knight. Who had done this to her? Who had murdered the man who had stolen her heart? She placed a hand flat against her stomach, holding herself together when her world threatened to fall apart.

King Aric lifted his distraught daughter into his arms, carrying her to her room. She stopped fighting halfway there, letting herself lie limp in his arms. There was no point without Aston. Aric set her on her bed and left the room, closing the door silently behind him.

Jade stayed where she was until her mother came to her, hours later. She was carrying a worn, leather sheath, a shining silver blade laid atop it. The sheath was stained with blood, undoubtedly Aston's. Whoever had murdered him had thrown it to his side, as if taunting him, saying he couldn't defend himself.

Jade looked at the queen as she floated closer but didn't sit up. "What do you want, Mother?" she asked. She wanted to be left alone with her thoughts, her memories. She wanted to be allowed to fade away into oblivion.

"Come now, Jade. It is not befitting a woman of your beauty to mourn so. You knew the man hardly three months. Surely he could not mean so much to you."

"I love him, Mother."

"You mean loved," Queen Margaret corrected.

Jade narrowed her gaze. "I mean love," she replied.

Her mother smiled, a subdued arch of her lips, before placing the bloody sheath on her bed. "Your father thought you might want this, though I'm not sure why," she said. She gave Jade a gentle hug, which the princess did not return. Her mother knew nothing of love. A forced marriage didn't show a woman her own heart.

"Thank you," she replied.

With a sigh, the queen stood and left. Jade pulled the sword into her lap, marveling at its weight and size. She lifted it, wrapping both hands around the hilt and allowing the shining blade to reach for her canopy. It made her forearms hurt, holding the sword up, but it was a nice hurt.

After another moment, she dropped the sword back down and slid it into its sheath. As she did, her bracelet caught the light. She allowed her lips a small smile as she pinched the silver sword charm between her fingers. She pulled her arm to her chest, wrapping the other around her stomach as she lay down again, allowing her tears to continue. She couldn't pretend nothing had happened, as her mother was. Her mother had known nothing of Aston. She hadn't even seen him alive! If her father died, would the queen mourn? Would she say nothing had changed?

Jade sat up again, eyeing the sheath at the end of her bed. What would Aston do, if he were there and she was gone? Would he sit around and cry, mourning her, or would he do something to avenge her? She took a look around her room, taking in the crystal horses she'd collected since she was a child, the pink canopy above her head, the matching silk comforter she was sitting on. She looked at her white wardrobe, still propped open from the day she'd left. Her wedding dress was hanging over her mirror, undoubtedly Matilda's doing.

Jade stood and walked to the mirror, picking up the dress and holding it over her body. If Aston were alive, they would be making plans to be married, right now. She would have a reason to wear the beautiful white gown. Instead, her mother would want her to go through with the original plans to marry Jacob. She shuddered at the thought.

She couldn't stay here. She had no life in this palace, this *country* anymore. Her life lay beyond the castle walls, in a little cabin in the woods. Her life lay stone cold in the palace somewhere, being prepared for a warrior's burial. Would King Donn and Prince Talbot take Aston back to Fridel with them to be buried? Would they return his body to his sister and father?

A soft knock at the door made Jade jump. She threw the wedding dress to the ground and returned to her bed before answering with a quiet, "You may enter."

Prince Talbot walked in. His broken arm hung limp in its sling, and his neck was bruised from where her brother had tried to kill him. Talbot walked to her, sitting beside her on the bed, which shocked her. Even Aston had been more formal around her to begin with.

The prince turned to her, then. His eyes were red and moist, his cheeks holding clear trails where his tears had fallen. Jade was surprised; the man had never seemed to care about Aston before, when he'd ruined his life. What had changed?

"I wanted to apologize to you, Princess Jade," he began. Jade nodded, encouraging him to continue. "I feel that this is my fault. If I hadn't.. if I could have.." Unsure of what to do, Jade patted Talbot's shoulder gently, careful not to jar his arm. Talbot reached up with his good hand and set it atop Jade's. "This isn't right. This isn't how it was supposed to end," he told her.

"I know, Talbot. I don't blame you."

"What will you do now?"

Jade looked away, thinking. She knew what she had to do. Could she trust Talbot? "I plan to leave Adion. I plan to never return, and I plan to find the person who killed Aston."

"Do you have any idea who could have done it?" Talbot asked her.

Jade nodded. "I have guesses. For now, I want to leave."

"Where will you go?"

"Back to Fridel, with Delgrab and Alys. I think they will have me, and someone has to tell them about Aston."

Talbot nodded his agreement. "I want to help," he announced.

Jade turned to look at him. "Excuse me?" she questioned.

"I want to help you. I want to find his killer, too. I want to be able to live with this guilt. I think this is what I am supposed to do."

Jade smiled at the prince. He had come so far since she had met him. He was a kind man now. He would make a great king. "What about your father?" she asked him.

Talbot shrugged. "What about him?"

Jade smiled and pulled Talbot into a hug before standing and going to her wardrobe. She grabbed a bag and quickly packed it. She would have laughed at the irony of the situation if she wasn't so sad.

"How do we go without being noticed?" Talbot asked her.

Jade glanced at her window and smiled. "I have an idea."

An hour later, she'd been to the throne room and retrieved Aston's satchel, telling her mother and father that she needed it to part with her feelings. Her father had objected, but the queen had been more than happy to allow Jade to take it. Now, she was climbing down the grey walls of the palace backwards, holding onto the rope from Aston's grappling hook. Talbot had gone through the palace and out the front door, his hurt shoulder not allowing him to climb down.

As soon as her feet touched the ground, Jade felt her heart lift a bit. She'd felt too cramped, being inside the palace. The place that had once been her home held nothing but bad memories. She turned to take one last look at it before blowing a kiss to the moss covered walls and to her knight, who was still somewhere inside. Then she turned and followed after Talbot, racing him to the stables. She tacked her horse slowly, watching as Sebastian helped Talbot tack Red and then gave the prince a hand up.

"Can you ride with one arm?" she questioned.

Talbot smirked at her. "How do you think I travelled here?" he answered.

Jade watched in awe as the prince maneuvered his big bay with his knees, holding the reins in only one hand. She smiled at him before finishing Sterling and mounting. Sebastian handed her Edward's reins as well, and she sadly smiled down at him.

"Leaving again, Princess Jade?" he asked her, a twinkle lighting up the old man's eyes.

Jade nodded and leaned down to kiss the man on his wrinkled cheek. "Thank you, Sebastian, again," she told him. She followed Talbot out of the stables and onto the path leading away from Adion. Talbot broke Red into a gallop and Jade followed, urging Sterling faster. Aston's satchel bounced against her back as she rode, and she felt comfortable, having him so close.

She vowed to herself that she would catch Aston's murderer or die trying. She was grateful to have Talbot to help her, and she knew Delgrab, Alys, and even little Richie would do all they could to help as well. She clung to Aston's sword, which she held in her lap, laid across the saddle, and smiled. She would learn to fight with the blade. She would become strong and agile, quick and sure-footed. This would be *her* weapon from now on. It had been chosen for her.

Chosen for her at her Knight's End.

About the Author

Jami Montgomery is a twenty-two year old author from South Texas. She spends every second she has writing, reading, and buying countless books. Chances are, if you can't find her, she is furiously typing away on her computer or buried in a book somewhere. Or lost in a bookstore.

Knight's End is Jami's first published work, and she looks forward to sharing more stories with her readers, family, and friends.

Made in the USA
Charleston, SC
05 September 2012